Your First
Love Affair
with SELF

YOUR FIRST LOVE AFFAIR WITH SELF

Rewrite Your Next Love Story
by turning your Pain into Purpose and Power
Spiritually, Personally, Professionally

PATRICIA Y. MCCULLOUGH-OLIVER

XULON PRESS

Xulon Press
2301 Lucien Way #415
Maitland, FL 32751
407.339.4217
www.xulonpress.com

Unless otherwise indicated, Scripture quotations taken
from the Holy Bible, New International Version (NIV).
Copyright © 1973, 1978, 1984, 2011 by Biblica, Inc.™.
Used by permission. All rights reserved.

Printed in the United States of America.

Paperback ISBN-13: 978-1-6322-1927-5
eBook ISBN-13: 978-1-6322-1928-2

OVERALL JOURNEY PRAYER

Dear Readers,

I pray you live with your hearts keenly focused on the ONE who LOVES you the most. I pray you live your life with HIM as your center! I pray your hearts are focused on eternity as you build HIS KINGDOM and live for the GLORY of GOD Alone!

I pray you KNOW and experience HIS LOVE in ways that overwhelm you with HIS presence. May your passion and love for Jesus empower you to LOVE others. – **Cassandra (Sandy) Woods**

THE AFFAIR

The *First Love Affair with SELF* is a braided story that follows a beautiful and affluent young women, Payton Jennings, whose life falls apart at the end of the relationship. Upon going on a cruise and encountering a mysterious figure, she winds up on a journey of self-discovery and self-love. Throughout the book, the author pauses to reflect upon her *own* past and offers bits of insight that may help readers along on their journey. Ultimately, understanding the process is as important as the destination. Waiting is powerful.

ACKNOWLEDGMENTS

I want to thank the Lord Jesus Christ for the inspiration and vision of this book. The Lord has *literally* guided my hand to tell this love story and share it with you. I want to thank my husband, Derrell L. Oliver, whom I know the Lord placed in my life long before I realized. He is one of the kindest, supportive, spirit-led men who lets me know daily how much he loves me and appreciated my support for him and our children. Thank you, honey bunn, for putting up with my over the top energy and overabundance desire for kisses. Thank you for your guidance in my life by always keeping me focused – well as best as you can. I love you, dearly. My son, Demetrius McCullough, thank you for being such a creative young man with much support, who always keeps me thinking and digesting *some* of your knowledge. I cannot wait for the release of your book. Caylan and Cameron Oliver, thank you guys for allowing me to be the bonus mom that God hand-picked just for this season in your lives. Shay McCullough my bonus and fit right in daughter. You are a gift from heaven. The best is yet to come for you all. Thank you, Stella and Aubrey Goodwin, for being parents who always stood by me and believed in the best for your children. Your marriage journey of 60+ years has been a book within itself. My sister Peggy Easter and niece Iliah Easter thanks for all the support during this writing process by giving me much to think about from different perspectives on relationships. Through the years, God blessed my life with some fantastic villages of friends at various stages of my Tear-formation. Cassandra (Sandy) Woods, you have been my sidekick and BFF for over 30 plus years. We have been through this Christian journey called life together, and you have been nothing but real and reliable, except not agreeing that I am the funnier of us two.

My village of friends Terry Ellis, Cassandra Steele, Pam Owens-Freeman, Debrah Mitchel, Phyllis Dickerson, Nancy Armstrong, Cecily Storm, Michele Wright, Shari Love-Davis, Judy Reed-Wells, Annette Basey, Turea Truttling-Flowers, Deun Ogunlana, Meddie Wilkins, Balinda Banks, Trudy Redus, Phanie Wicks, Tami East, Jerelyn Duncan and Dezette Weathers thank you so much. You all have been there through the years and dropped many support avenues when I needed you the most. Even though our life journey has taken us in different directions, you all are still some of my biggest cheerleaders. My Big Girl -girlfriends, Timmons, Mrs. Irean Ducket, Irean Perkins, Jane Bogan, Glenda Bates, Stephanie Stallworth, Claudette Votor, Vivian Jones, Linda Gillium-Ware, Yvonne Harris, Nettie Pearl Stewart and Earlean Levert just know you are some exceptional women. Ladies, thanks to all of you for the wisdom you've shared with me personally and professionally through the years. All I know is that everyone needs to be blessed from your wisdom and guidance you've bestowed to me. To all of you, no longer here with me physically. I know you are still here, spiritually. Grandmother Effie Howell, Mrs. Evelyn Ellis, Aunt Joe Ann Howell, Kay Cotton, Sareta Phillips, Aunt Eursla, Aunt Shirley Goodwin, Aunt Ernest Pam, Aunt Gladis, Aunt Willie Bell, and Fannie Curry, thank you guys for just being women used for God's glory in my life. How I wish you were still here; women need you in their lives today. To my Godchildren, Destini Hunt, Roberta Woods, River Storm, and Ramesses Banks you are amazing young women and men. Look out everyone here they come on a mission to change the world. Just keep seeking the Lord first and he will add all things unto you. Love you guys.

TABLE OF CONTENTS

INTRODUCTION

This book will help you learn how to have your first love affair with Self at any age. These basic principles will help you with every relationship in your personal and professional life by depositing valuable insight into your relationships through Payton's experience. During this journey, I want you to reconnect with hope, purpose, and a desire to come from under toxic relationships and move to a healthier emotional connection with yourself. Learning how to embrace your true love story, even the painful pages of your reality will be your mission. After reading this book, it is my desire for you to walk into a better understanding of loving yourself deeper and more fulfilling than ever before. Change happens from the inside out; therefore, this process is the only way you will be able to rewrite your personal love story. In your relationships, work at getting to know the individual's *STORY* to not disrupt your *HISTORY*. Your responsibility for this journey is to become a vessel that God can use.

Payton will be on a mission to better understand herself with a desire to change the path of her toxic relationships. She believed doing so will help her become a better person for and to herself.

You will go along on a journey with Payton when she ventures on a cruise. She will find solace and become engulfed by the peace received from the waters at sea. Her mission will be exploring many parts of the country searching for inner peace. On this cruise, she will meet a wise elderly lady who has some interesting ties to the cruise liner. This is a woman of strength—a spiritual mentor who so many wish they had encountered in the early years of their relationships. This mentor has an abundance of BIG girl wisdom to share with Payton and you on this cruise. She is wise with much to share from her early years of making mistakes in her relationships. While sharing the process of self-discovery and all the life lessons she learned along the way about love, Payton will often *try* to get back in touch with Lady Von Kisser to share updates on the relationship wisdom she is receiving with various individuals on her journey.

PRELUDE

P ayton was on cloud nine one breathtaking evening, but then the thought of her man, River, hit her spirit. *He is out traveling this week again. Hum, I need to feel close to him right now. I need to feel his arms around me. If I can't be with him physically, at least I can try to be with him emotionally as she quivered within her body.* She wanted to feel that feeling again—that feeling that made her body entertain those warm thoughts when they were together. She decided the closest place she could go to feel his presence was their special place on the wall, by the water, off Lake Shore Drive. As she walked towards her destination, many people were still running, walking, and biking around the lake.

Lord, I thank you, she thought as she moved into that direction of their special place. *I never thought I would feel this way about a person in my life again. I know, I know. I have said this on many occasions about the other men in my life, but this one, this one right here. I feel like this is the one.*

I believe this is the one Lord. Even though River believes our timing is off, he often says, 'Perfect us, imperfect, me, blah, blah, blah.'

As she moved closer to their special spot, the location was already occupied by a couple hugged up. A little smile lit her face because she knew that feeling, oh so well. She moved toward a spot, a few feet from the couple down the wall where she could still hear their soft voices and see the lighthouse across the waters that they so often gazed at together snuggled up.

She secured her spot then stood there with her eyes closed and enjoyed the night breeze. The sound of the water blended with the sound of bikes and light chatter gave her much comfort and joy in her spirit. Payton propped herself up on the wall with her eyes closed, still in that moment of reflecting on her growing love for this amazing man that the Lord had blessed her with. Boom! Along with a scream startled her, causing her to miss the wall. Snapping her eyes open, she grabbed the wall to brace herself from falling. Payton laughed at herself, wondering how she looked to the others around her. She gazed around and her eyes landed upon the couple from earlier. What appeared before her in slow motion took her somewhere dark. It was as if her eyes were trying to protect her from the images. Trying to sort out what she was seeing, it took a minute for her eyes to get focused on the couple. The side view of the man on the wall was not just any man. This was *her* man. She froze; she gasped, her mouth moved, but nothing came out. A pounding started in her heart like someone was hitting her in the middle of her chest with a hammer. There it was again—that pain, a pain that no one should ever experience. She felt that pain she never wanted to feel again—the pain in your being that makes your heart beat so fast, you feel as if it is coming out of your chest. The pain that forces you to fight for air as your chest holds a no move position. Yeah, that pain. "Perfect us, imperfect me." River was saying their words, the same words, to the other woman. Payton stared out over the lake as tears formed in her eyes then streamed down her face.

"Perfect us, imperfect me." Continued to echo across the waters and in her thoughts.

Rage and fear embraced her heart and tears embraced her soul. She looked back over the lake and stared at the lighthouse thinking about her dream that had just evaporated out into the water.

"How did I get here AGAIN?" she said under her breath as she felt herself fainting.

YOU-Discovery

Author's Notes

And so it began, Payton's journey to a you-discovery that so many individuals at some point in their lives should take began that day. I invite you to join us. It will allow you to discover self-love and evaluate your relational experiences in your life. Once you realize there is one constant variable in all your relationships and that variable is you, then and only then will your journey towards a healthy, nurturing relationship begin to move forward. Many times, you are busy trying to convince people you are important while secretly fearing you are not. Learn and understand that no one, and I do mean no one, will value what you don't value.

So, get excited because you are going to take a much-needed cruise by yourself, for yourself while digging deep within yourself. The caviar is that you are going to start

1

with a clean slate; yes, you get to build your desired relationships with yourself and others from the ground up. Understand you will have to make some major decisions and follow-through to not only see a reformation but the transformation toward a better you.

There will be work on this cruise. For this journey, you will need to write, reflect, and renew. Some will say, "I do not do the journal thing." If that sounds like you, I suggest writing when needed. C.S. Lewis, one of the most influential Christians of the twentieth century, kept a journal until he was converted. Through the years, writing my thoughts helped me self-examine my prayers and rewrite my personal love story. You will also meet some interesting people with scenarios you have gone through or are going through. These relationships are from their personal and professional perspective.

You may be in a situation that is not living up to the desires you seek. All I ask is that you digest this information and implement the new behaviors. I want you to reflect on what you are inputting into your relationships. Most of you are sitting back just waiting and hoping to have a good relationship. Some are playing the blame game. Decide to make changes. But most important, along the way, make some positive deposits in your relationship with others. I make it a point that in any of my relationships, I want to be remembered for what I have deposited into them.

Reflection:

Write a letter to yourself about your relationship (the truth).

(Ex) Hey, stop acting like you have the perfect relationship when you don't. Relationship, you let me down a lot. So what if it is my fault most of the time? Ok, my relationships with __ is not what people think it is.

Another Man, My Man

Payton

On a cool autumn evening, Payton left her office in Chicago and decided to take a drive. She was loving life, driving her dream car, a Bianco Maserati Quattroporte SQ4, down the Lake Shore drive strip. Being excited about what was going on in her life was an understatement. Recently, she was appointed to the position of ambassador of leadership for a country, and four of her books were on the New York Times Bestselling list for the past five years. One of her books was in production for a Hallmark, movie. She had traveled the world on the speaking circuits and on top of that, she landed the contract of a lifetime in Abu Dhabi for her company. Payton was a proud owner of a beautiful two-story penthouse condo overlooking the lake, a wine cellar, and a world-class jazz collection that she created over the years. Payton appealed to the eyes, and when she walked into a room, she became the room. She had a personality that many simultaneously admired, envied, and despised from afar. Most would say she had that "TP" factor, the "total package." Payton was living her best life, at least it appeared that way to others. Unfortunately, through the years, she had developed a pattern of toxic relationships in her career and personal life. She often felt that something must be wrong with others because no one understood her and the ups and downs in her behavior. She never allowed herself to be close to anyone because she was not interested in people's opinions or observations about her life decisions. Deep down, truth be told, she didn't want to face her truth or her reality. Payton was a wounded vessel, and some would say a broken spirit full of scars, scabs, and sores. The wounds left scar marks on her heart, scabs that healed on the top but were still too painful to talk about on the inside, and sores that were still open wounds for all to see. At this juncture in Payton's life, she thought she had it all, especially since the man of her dreams and desires had entered her life. Or should we say ANOTHER MAN?

As she cruised down Lake Shore Drive, she burned with a desire to get to the water's edge. Water had such a special effect on her life. It gave her spirit a sense of peace, warmth, life, energy, and security, but on the other hand, her flesh felt fear, lack of control, and insecurity. She let the top down and allowed the wind to blow through her hair and on her face. *This feeling has to be close to heaven*, she thought. The atmosphere took her to places of inner passion and excitement. It was that new love feeling that washes over you when someone has touched your heart. The thoughts of passion took her visually and emotionally to their private times together. His hands, his mouth, his tongue—she could still feel his touch all over her body. How could she be so blessed to have a man of this caliber in her life who was always in her thoughts?

Their encounter happened earlier that year at one of her many networking functions in Chicago. When their eyes met, there was an intensity of knowing him that seeped into the crevices of her soul. Magic, just pure magic, was exposed. Before words were spoken, the chemistry smacked her straight in her face. Her heart met him before her eyes could catch sight and focus on the presence of perfection. She knew he had the finest tailors. His clothing spoke money and left no room for the imagination, as the garments sculpted his body. His caramel skin was flawless, as if he wore makeup. His short curly hair made you want to experience running your hands over his scalp. A baby-fine beard shadowed his face with the hand of an artist. Pearly white teeth looked as if he invested a fortune on his mouth. When he spoke, his vernacular had world traveler oozing from his loins. His air of confidence made him stand out among most. As the principal owner of a successful hedge fund company, he was powerful and extremely comfortable financially. This Adonis did all the right things and said all the right words as the relationship grew in the right direction. In the beginning, he made it clear that with his traveling schedule and demands of his career, he was not interested in a serious relationship. The conversation was so clear to Payton because he said it often: "Perfect us, imperfect me." Flexibility without insecurities was all he had to offer. A non-committed relationship was ok, so she thought, excepted, and wanted to believe.

She said one thing with her mouth, but her heart felt something totally different. This was a safe place for her. It kept her from realizing that she may not be the one he wanted to be with as his final destination for a life partner. She believed she could protect her heart from pain.

They did not get together regularly because of his schedule, but when they did, there were provocative and detailed conversations about what a future would look like. He wanted to know how many children she desired, what made her happy, romantic dining, and passionate encounters. Engaging in sexual activities was the norm. She led herself to believe these encounters were ok, knowing the Lord would forgive her for her sins. This action was justified because he would be her husband one day; she prayed and knew this.

> *How we make excuses to fit our spiritual walk. Practicing sin is a behavior that turns into your lifestyle of sin. Stop talking the Christian life and start walking and living your beliefs. Stop living the carnal life.* -Patricia Y. McCullough-Oliver

Deep down, she believed if anyone could change his mind on their relationship, it would be her when that time presented itself. Believing this was easy for her flesh because he often shared with her how no one made him feel the way she did, how he could be himself with her, and he told her often he loved her and needed her in his life. Statements like that made her inhale and exhale with such heartfelt emotions.

> *Some of these statements are many men's mantras. If they show you their heart, at least the one they want you to believe, then you would do almost anything for them and most of you do. I'm not saying that there is no truth to the statements.*

> *But the truth is subjective; it depends on where they are in their lives. Many say these mantras and put you on a shelf until they are finished playing around and some never come back.* – *Patricia Y. McCullough-Oliver*

He took her places physically and emotionally that she had never experienced: holding hands while walking on beaches all over the world, courtside seats at major sports events, and other upscale events. He seldom took her to public settings in their city; he had others and didn't want them to cross paths. Introducing her as his special friend made her feel wanted and special. Her thoughts were, at least he recognizes me as special. When they were together, he never answered the phone when someone would call; he would let it go to voicemail even when the calls would come in at 2:00 a.m. *What a gentleman, he is not allowing anyone to disturb us,* Payton thought. There were times when her spirit didn't feel good about certain situations. At those times, she would push the thoughts out of her mind. There were also times when he would talk on the phone, but she noticed he would wait until she was not around. She would catch him talking and knew his mannerism when he talked to other women. But she would not give it a second thought because she knew he would not do that to her. He called her every day, all day. "He is so attentive; he could not possibly have time for someone else," she would say. Until that heartbreaking night by the lake hearing, as those words were spoken to someone else, "Perfect us, Imperfect me."

I know women who had said they were lying right beside the men when they were talking to their wives or significant other. So, don't allow that to be a safety net for your security in a relationship. Your safety net is your discernment spirit. Also, the title special friend is subjective. Most people that they will introduce you to already know the real special friend, and its not you. Ladies, the interviews that I have had with women solidify these statements – Patricia Y. McCullough-Oliver

Author's Notes

When do you stop living consciously and living outside of common sense? Start making conscious decisions to live a conscious life. Ask yourself, what does it mean to live a conscious life? I am glad you're asking that question as you're reading. It means seeing things as they are and not what you desire it to be. In the Christian community, we say you are walking in the flesh and not the spirit. When we don't live conscious lives, our decision making is off balance. Our goals should always be to learn from the decisions of our personal experience and then evaluate. There is a saying that experience is the best lesson. I will respectfully disagree. John Maxwell said, "Evaluated experience is the best lesson." Payton never wants to skip evaluating her relationships again and be forced to ask herself the question: How did I get here again?

A Lost Soul

Payton

Payton Jennings—talented, highly educated, full of energy, with many charismatic attributes. Coming up, she was well-bred with social status from her father's side of the family. Many of her character traits came from a mother who worked hard to fit into the elite's environment of superficiality. Payton was a hopeless romantic who often found herself in toxic, unfulfilling relationships in her personal and professional life. Payton was a lost soul that had no idea she was lost. She knew she was seeking something, but what, she had no idea. On the outside, she appeared to have it all together, but on the inside, she was a vessel full of emptiness. Her life was spiraling out of control. Just last week Payton was leaving the office of P.M.O Consulting Firm for the very last time. It was a day that was just the beginning of more disappointments to come. A year ago, she was living her dream and the desired life most envied. She was appealing to the eyes but needed much adjusting in the personality arena. Always playing the blame game, she manipulated the few friends she had. She often had a competing and envious spirit. These were characteristics that often-followed Payton through the years. She had developed a pattern of toxic relationships in her career and personal life. And on this day, it all came to a head. Being in an extremely competitive and backstabbing industry as a personal development consultant, Payton was known for displaying a bad attitude and aggressive tone with others. She didn't work well with coworkers or figureheads. She had an attitude of knowing it all with a nonnegotiable disposition. On many occasions, she often talked down to other managers and colleagues in the company to make herself look better than most. On this day, Payton was called in the office by the general manager and HR and to her surprise, the vice president of the company was in attendance. She was being written up for her inappropriate behavior and would be put on a P.I.P., (Personal Improvement Plan). In this situation, Payton voiced her unsolicited opinion too loudly and allowed the environment she was raised in display its ugly head too many times. Payton was often seen pointing her fingers in other's faces, speaking over people, not being a team player, and giving bad customer service to clients. That day, she was not only asked to leave the company but had to be escorted out of the building. Of course, it was not her fault. The people there were just very incompetent and insecure about her talent and the money her client list was bringing to the company. If they really knew all she had gone through in her life—health issues, losing people close to her at an early age, losing friends that she thought were her friends, bad boyfriends, and toxic relationships, they would've given her grace until she completely healed. After all, no one can put a timetable on the healing process she believed.

As she drove home from the office, she received a call from her girlfriend, a call she was dreading. Their relationship was complicated. Payton often felt there were too much competition and jealousy in the friendship. *She wants to have my life and often talks behind my back to others, never satisfied with herself,* Payton thought. Her girlfriend was too holy for her and judgmental at the same time, always talking to her about forgiveness, learning from others, and being a team player. But on this night during the phone conversation, her friend decided she didn't want to continue with their toxic friendship anymore. She would continue to lift Payton up in prayer from a distance. Payton felt that not all friendships were for a lifetime and that there were seasons to everything. Payton felt ok with the loss because she was cleaning out her emotionally draining surroundings. She would often say, "Too many of my friends have such a toxic existence anyway. They are holding me back. I know that some better friends will better understand me and admire all my abilities."

Author's Notes

In the Maxwell Leadership Bible, John Maxwell says, "We will never grow beyond four fundamental human needs. Sense of Worth: if missing, we feel inferior. Sense of Belonging: if missing, we feel insecure. Sense of Purpose: if missing, we feel illegitimate. Sense of Competence: if missing, we feel inadequate." We must settle these issues with God before we can come to a place of growth with ourselves.

I have learned through the years of my life journey that many individuals don't like themselves because they are living such deceptive lives. Therefore, they can't possibly like anyone else. Sure, we see many individuals at functions with their Jaeger-LeCoultre watches, Christian Louboutin red bottom shoes, and the finest of the finest designer bags. They make their grand entrance with their man, and sometimes someone else's man. We now own Bentleys, corporations, hedge funds, and multiple homes. Yet, with all the material accessories, women are traveling the world full of emptiness and putting themselves in position to the highest bidder. I see women now, no longer satisfied with six digits, but seeking seven digits and will sell their souls in the process for temporary passion. The only way they can relate to their counterpart is by belittling them to others to clear out the competition. There are high profile couples: power couples who are miserable with each other. It's a good look for others to believe they have it all together. For those who have walked in those shoes know that all that glitter and shine is not real gold or real diamonds; it's just LAB made everything. There is a saying that I often use, "You see the glory, but you don't know the story." Believe me, there is a story in all of us, and they are always relationship-centered. I know because I lived it. In my single days, I lived it, I traveled it, I experienced it. The jet-set life I called it back then. My relationships ran the gamut of powerful, and wealthy. I could go on, but this information is only for the purpose of me telling you I have walked away from it all on many occasions. My father had a lot to do with that behavior. He had a couple of rules that saved my life in relationships. One was if you ever need anything and you can't purchase it yourself, ask me and your mom. Second, no one gives you things without wanting something in return, especially a man. Very few men will convince themselves that they want nothing in return but when the romance ends, then you will see the real person. Everything has a price. Also, my saving grace was that I had a fellowship and a relationship with the Lord. I knew my market value. I couldn't be bought because there was no price tag associated with me. Many thought this, becasue of the way I carried myself. No, I didn't disrespectfully carry myself; I didn't have my first kiss until I was seventeen. My reasoning was I knew what I was bringing to the table. It was not material; it was priceless. My body was not for everyone, period. Later in years, my girlfriends could not understand how I could be in one good relationship with all the perks, end it, and be in another *good one.* Be careful with your definition of a good relationship or man. My definition of a good man was different from others and probably yours. My good man had nothing to do with finances and power. It had everything to do with the character and their spiritual walk. That is why it was easy to walk away from the gold and glitter. I knew all too well how empty that life felt. I had observed, experienced, and watched too many women live and try to endure that empty lifestyle. Please understand I am not saying being with someone who provides a certain lifestyle is bad. God has ordained the husband as the provider. Just keep it in the correct order for a better ending—the foundation and then the stuff it allows. Your source is coming from the Lord Jesus Christ. His world, His stuff. Ecclesiastes says nothing physical touches the soul, for the soul alone belongs to God and only He can fulfill those inner needs I'm paraphrasing. When you are good and clear on that, you won't continue to walk in "stuff without substance." You will desire something deeper within your soul other than material things.

Amen

18

The Big Lie - The Big Mess

<u>Payton</u>

Payton felt since the world was not appreciating her and her talents, she would take some much-needed time off. She decided to take a cruise to get out and see the world from a different perspective. Life was too short to sit back and entertain all the people who didn't get her vision or appreciate her wealth of knowledge. For the men who didn't appreciate good women, she would show them. Payton made up her mind that she would not allow herself to love again. She would not buy the t-shirt, "How did I get here again?" After all, "I can't get hurt if I don't put myself in that position again." All of this was said with such bitterness and pain in her heart. Her mission in life now was to protect her heart. Besides, she felt she was not missing anything anyway. Reality TV was not just for the big screen; it was her life...a BIG lie and a BIG mess.

> **When we experience pain most of the time, it is a symptom of something else that is going on in our life that must be healed first. It takes a very strong person to decide that they will go through the process of hurting and feel alone with the pain to heal. Emotions good and bad can create wholeness in one's life.** - *Patricia Y. McCullough-Oliver*

Laying her wardrobe out for travel that morning she put on her finest. "Navy is what I will sport for the cruise." She pulled out her blue Christian Louboutin, known as " Sammy-red bottoms shoes, St. John vintage navy and white pantsuit, and a few pieces of her signature jewelry: a GIA certified 5.53 platinum diamond ring along and Piaget Rose brooch. Wearing all of this weighed her down physically and emotionally. As Payton walked towards the embarkation and then the gangway of the cruise liner headed to the Middle East, her feet were having a toxic painful relationship with her legs. In between the pain she questioned the purchases. Although red bottoms were cute, every pair she owned hurt her feet and her gait was no longer cute in them. Payton had to find a place to sit down quickly and in a hurry. The ship was very crowded, and there was nothing in the eye's view.

"Lord we have not because we ask not," Payton said. "I need a place of rest."

And as if the Red Sea opened at her command, two beautiful royal purple seats appeared in the corner. After she found her way to one of the seats, she quickly laid her head back to rest her eyes for a second.

Out of nowhere, she heard this voice. "Hi pretty girl, pretty girl," the angelic voice said.

When she opened her eyes slowly, she appeared. The first thing Payton noticed was her beautiful violet brooch and unusual scent, natural but different, and a meek woman with a strong presence.

"May I sit here with you?"

Before Payton could speak, the woman made herself comfortable in the second royal purple chair and began sharing some ever-changing knowledge with Payton about her life.

"I was led in my spirit to come and talk with you," she said. This lady shared information about her toxic relationships, personal and professional. This surprised Payton because she barely knew the woman, but there was something mystical about her. A desire rose within Payton to want more out of her relationships. Even envious feelings that she could not explain came over her. Payton had never experienced a feeling of jealousy, at least any jealousy that she would admit. In the process of getting to know her, she found out the woman's name was Lady Von Kisser. Her spirit was safe and free, but it had a deep soul. She came to know that Von Kisser was a wealthy woman who had traveled the world and had her share of relationships, both positive and negative.

"Payton there were two principles I had to master and live by," said Von Kisser. "To continue to have self- love and understanding the me, I was destined to be. Once I mastered them, I experienced my first love affair. My first love affair was an affair with myself, which allowed me to rewrite my love story.

Von Kisser told Payton a story about a life of many relationships where she faced daily emotional and physical abuse until she finally met *them*. Von Kisser never went into who "them" were, but she said they changed her life forever.

Payton asked, "Why did you stay in toxic relationships so long?"

"Because I valued the relationship with the people more than I valued or loved myself. I followed my heart and not my spirit. Until you are willing to have that honest conversation with God about yourself in relationships, you will never know the peace of God or your purpose in God's kingdom for yourself. I hid my pain from the world, but more sadly, I hid it from myself. I believed I could mask it with superficial things. I learned the hard way, you can't solve an inward problem with an outward solution."

Lady Von Kisser went on to elaborate. "I was a rider, a ride and die girl in my relationships who didn't know when or how to get off. The problem was, I had no idea what a good man or love looked like, my dear. I allowed someone else's definition of a good man to become my idea of one and later my reality of one. I presented and told others I had a satisfied and beautiful life. I lived a life that I wanted others to believe. I lived THE LIE I wanted them to see, the life I crafted. I just had no idea who I was. I was a victim of that 'the me I want to be' mentality. I wanted people to believe my life was amazing. The problem was, I was not being the me that the Lord had predestined for me to be. Most of my life, I did not care what God wanted for my life because I never asked Him."

"What were you afraid of?" asked Payton.

Suddenly the atmosphere got quiet, and her words came out of her mouth very slowly. "I was afraid of what God might have led me to do or become. What if it was something that I did not want to do or be? What if God wanted me to be with someone who didn't have the lifestyle I desired to live?"

She held Payton in her gaze for a short period. Her look was an expression Payton had never seen before; it was as if she stopped breathing.

Author's Notes

In John Ortberg's bestselling book *The ME I Want to BE*, he shares some amazing insights on the concept called the me I want to be mentality. He expounds on the "me" we don't want to be, pretend to be, think we should be, other people want us to be, afraid to be, fail to be, meant to be, and most importantly the "me" that God has predestined me to be. My goodness, and we wonder why so many individuals have no idea who they are, living a life of emptiness with no peace.

Ortberg believes if there was not a mirror of what others told us about ourselves, there would be parts of us we would never see because we subconsciously do not want to know or see the real us. We know ourselves better than anyone else, but on the other hand, no one knows you worse than yourself. Why? Because we embellish, justify, forget, and sometimes not realize we are doing it. However, for some, they know exactly what they are doing.

Carol Tavris and Elliot Aronson's book *Mistakes Were Made (But Not by Me)* charts the mental tricks we play to deceive ourselves. We all fall for the self-serving biases. We claim too much credit and too little blame. Our memories are not simply faulty; they are faulty in favor of our ego.

God does not mass produce. He handcrafts each one of us individually. Your path to growth will not always be like others. It will be difficult at times. Your responsibility is to become the vessel that God can use for his kingdom. I see so many people, especially women, trying to live someone else's life. Not just admiring but cutting their throats trying to stake existence. The women that have experienced those lifestyles will tell you. The grass isn't greener on the other side. It has some expensive yard furniture and artificial grass, but it is anything but nicer. There are some amazing actresses out there but after a while, what goes on in the dark will come to light.

Ortberg shares we must learn to find our identity by learning why God created you. Once you spend time with yourself second and God first, you will realize what you want isn't any particular outcome on any particular project. Those are all just means to an end. What you want is to be fully alive inside. What we want is the inner freedom to live in love and joy. When I read this, it was so right on point with the decision I made later in my life. I sought the feeling of being alive inside and peaceful living. I got out of the toxic surroundings, people of superficial social arenas, and stopped caring if people liked me or not. It is amazing what you learn when you are observing from the outside. You stop looking and start seeing, you start listening and stop talking. I heard this saying so often, and I have lived by it. The most important task of our lives is not what we do but what we become. It is not what we leave here on earth for people, but what we leave inside of people that will have the greatest impact. I learned to not focus on leaving an inheritance but a legacy. I am aware the inheritance will make for a comfortable lifestyle. Unfortunately, some children will never appreciate the sacrifices that went into providing for their future. inheritance. Saying all of that, I had to get to that thought process myself. Ladies, you will never find yourself until you face the truth with or about yourself. In Kelly Johnson's book, EMERGE! She talks about you are a masterpiece. There is a question that she puts on the table. Do you view yourself as God's masterpiece? Kelly challenges you to stop focusing on the bad of yourself and focus on the good.

I lived a certain lifestyle in my early years. I did a talk on my life called "Living the lifestyle of the rich and famous though I had it going on, but I was miserable." I laugh when I think about that talk and the long, crazy title. Oh, the ending of the speech: Nothing, I had nothing but emptiness. Like King Solomon says in Ecclesiastes, empathy, empathy, empathy it's all empathy. Only God knows our full potential, and He is guiding us towards the best version of ourselves all the time.

In college, I was known as the "no" woman and Stonewall Jackson, who was a general in the American Civil War with a hard and cold disposition. I laugh at this also when I think about how guys saw me. No one was having me mentally or physically. At the time, this had nothing to do with my Christian walk. I just always knew I was different. I could not explain this behavior. At an early age, I knew my body was special, and it was not just for anybody. I have been a track and field girl since the age of eleven and received numerous athletic scholarships from D1 universities. In college, I would get compliments on my appearance, athletic abilities, the way I carried myself, and personality. The crazy thing is I would get offended. I'll explain in a few. Just keep reading.

I recall when I rededicated my life to Christ and came back to college after spring break. I looked in my dorm room mirror, and for the first time, I saw myself. I saw my eyes through God's eyes. I had such a glow that I had never seen before. I told myself this is what people are seeing. The Holy Spirit started speaking to me. I knew this was the first time I was hearing the Lord's voice. He said, "Now you see me as I see you. It's your inner beauty that they see that outshines the temporal appearance as the world sees." That day was the beginning of me learning about who I really was and genuinely loving myself. When I realized I had something special about me that lived on the inside, the compliments did not bother me anymore. I knew it was not just the physical me that they were seeing, it was also, Christ that lived within me. How does this translate? People were drawn to Christ, not just me. One thing I do know is there is a pretty baby girl born every day. If you think your beauty or bubbling personality is going to keep anyone in your life permanently, you are going to live a disappointed and unsatisfied life. Transformation happens from the inside out.

Reflection: Identify your ME's Example: Me's: want to be, pretend to be, others want you to be, afraid to be, fail to be, predestined to be through God's predestination (seek him to find the answers).

Payton

As Payton continued to enjoy the conversation, she noticed Lady Von Kisser stopped talking and looked at her differently. "Is there a problem?"

"It can be," said Lady Von Kisser.

"You are listening, but you are not hearing from me."

Payton thought that to be strange because she was looking at her in the eyes. "I don't understand."

"I pray you will one day, my child. I pray that you will meet THEM one day."

Payton felt funny again, and her feet still throbbed from earlier. She knew that she needed to check-in and head to her cabin before she passed out, but she wanted to ask her about who "Them" were.

"Oh my, I do tend to ramble off at the mouth, but there was something about your spirit that I felt drawn to." Von Kisser took a deep breath. "You are seeking something, my child, and often looking in all the wrong places."

Payton gave her a crooked smile, a smile that gave her a little chill because she knew deep down that was a true statement but wondered how this woman she just met knew this about her. Payton, like most, had no idea what she was seeking. Most of the time she felt it was too late in life to turn around. Too old, too tired, and don't care anymore.

The two decided to have dinner later that night to finish the conversation. Deep down in Payton's spirit, she felt something amazing would happen, but she could not put her finger on it. It was just this feeling. Lately, she had been having these feelings quite often but just shrugged them off.

THE LOVE AFFAIR

Payton had slept longer than she anticipated, so she ran a little late to dinner with Lady Von Kisser. "Oh, how I pray that she doesn't think I'm rude for coming in late."

As she approached the Lido deck for dinner, she could not resist going outside to see the beautiful waters. As she pressed her body to the rail and allowed the wind to pass through her hair and on her face, a feeling came over her—a feeling she was familiar with, oh so well. He had become a part of her life mentally and physically. He would hold her hostage in the bed sometimes for days. He would not tell her when he was coming, nor would he tell her how long he would be staying. He would just show up and sometimes stay too long. He would disguise himself in other forms, but she knew him as soon as she felt him. His name was Lonely.

When Payton was a little girl, many times she did not fit in and felt lonely. Not lonely because she was not liked but a loneliness that did not empower her. She was not happy, and should have been. She really could not explain it back then. She had a hole within her like something was missing. A loneliness that said, 'I think there is something more, and I just do not know what it is.' She would often layout in front of her home on the grass and talk to the sky. She always felt so much peace at the time. She did not realize that she was talking to the Lord. She had not dedicated her life to Christ at that time. But when she did start living for Him all she knew was that it felt peaceful, like someone was listening to her and the hole disappeared. But, as of late that hole was showing up again.

Payton finally made her way back inside for dinner.

"Oh, young lady, I'm so glad that you could make it," Lady Von Kisser said.

"I am so sorry, the time just got away from me. I strayed outside to admire the view and the water. It was so amazing."

"Yes, it is, Payton. That is your name?"

"Yes. it is," said Payton.

"You must excuse me, this mind of mine has been coming and going for years. It seems that I have been on this boat most of my life, it's as if I got on it and never left," she said as she stared off in space with that expression that Payton observed earlier.

This time Payton gave her a strange look.

"Payton sweetheart, please tell me a little about yourself. I talked so much the first time we met. I didn't give you a chance to tell me about yourself. I can't put my finger on it, but there seems to be such a spirit of unhappiness and hurt that shadows you, young lady."

Payton told her all about her life, but she was a little annoyed by her statement about her spirit. She went on about working in the real world and how so many people were jealous of her and her success.

"People often tell me that I don't listen," said Payton.

She chuckled because those were the same words that Lady Von Kisser said to her earlier. Lady Von Kisser raised one eyebrow.

"I do listen all the time. I just don't feel they know what they are talking about. I get so tired of married men hitting on me or me being attracted to them. I get into dysfunctional relationships but cannot get out. My relationships do not last or have much meaning anymore. The minute I express my feelings, they leave. I give my all, I am a ride or die girl and I have the best personality in the United States of America. Well, I do tend to demand and complain a bit much I have been told, but I deserve to have it all. I love my life even if I do not have many people to share it with. I just do not like people. I do not have time for them especially the ones that don't agree with my outlook on life. We are just on different levels. I know I need to work on being nicer, but I just do not have time for that. You know how people can be."

Lady Von Kisser looked at her in amazement and boredom as Payton talked about how amazing she was and the wonderful life she was living. Lady Von Kisser kept her mouth closed as long as she could. "Well, Ms. Payton always remember it's nice to be important, but it's more important to be nice."

The one thing that Lady Von Kisser knew is it's not what people say, it's what they don't say, and Payton was saying a lot of nothing. "I bet she is the only one who thinks she is so amazing," Lady Von Kisser said to herself.

"Ms. Von Kisser, Ms. Von Kisser," said Payton.

"Oh, I'm sorry young lady, you have to excuse me. Sometimes my mind wanders," she said with a little smirk.

Payton continued, "You know, I know that the Lord will bless me one day with the right kind of man. I will just have to be patient. I have money, a career—" she said under her breath. "I'm not bad on the eye. I keep my body in tip-top shape. What else could a man want? I'm here, come get me." Payton laughed. Then it hit her. She was the only one laughing.

"What is the matter, Ms. Von Kisser?"

The pause before she spoke was so long that Payton became a little uncomfortable.

Lady Von Kisser leaned into Payton and said, "There will come a day when you will realize that you have not been truthful with yourself in such a very long time. You know there is one thing that I do know. People have made up lies about themselves for so long that they forget the truth. I wonder if you remember the truth," said Lady Von Kisser." You could have bought Payton with a dime, not really. I bet you could have bought her for less.

Authors Notes

We will never be able to love people correctly until we see them clearly through God's eyes, then we can appreciate them completely. Many will never get to this point because people live a life of untruths."

"If someone asked you about your past, how honest would you be about your life Payton? Would you leave out some important details? Would you pretend it was something that it was not? You will either feed your history or your destiny. Which one is growing in your life? We cannot outdistance the past. The truth always wins." Lady Von Kisser held Payton in her gaze to see if she would respond.

PAIN TO POWER PRINCIPLE

<u>Author's Notes</u>

Coming to grips with the truth, rooted in the past, is the greatest source to power.- Keith Ablow, MD

Many women live in denial. How do you know you are living in denial? Von Kisser went on to tell Payton how she would tell people that her life was nearly perfect. Just listen to people when they talk about their lives. Again, it is not what they say. It is what they do not say. She wore all the correct attire, drove all the latest vehicles, attended the correct functions. All was well on the outside, but the inside was a different story. She had been married for over twenty years in her first marriage. Sometimes, she wondered whether drinking a glass of wine or two to get to sleep was becoming a problem. Her justification was plenty of people did not sleep well and used wine for comfort. And yes, there was also the way she went on shopping sprees to lift her mood. She did not have much interest in sex anymore nor her husband. After all, she had lived with the same man for nearly two decades, which is not exactly the ultimate recipe for passion . He was known to put his hands-on women in other relationships, but that did not phase her until he put his hands on her. She led herself to believe it was not that bad because this did not happen often. She made sure she never took him to that point. Do not be a victim in your own life. The God you serve is not controlled by conditions because he controls the conditions. Even though God is in control, you may have to go through something to get to something that the Lord is taking you to. The Israelites getting to the Promised Land was not easy. Romans 8:28 says, "And we know that all things work together for good to those who love God and those who are called according to his purpose." But, know this, all things may not be good as you go through, but it will be for your good as it is being worked out. You can prosper during these turbulent times. Just trust the process. Von Kisser said she learned to make her pain her power. She said to Payton, "No human being in your life gets the final word on who God has made you to be or has destined your life to become." What we can't do is let the life you have to distract you from the life you want.

Look at your pain as a process of getting to the purpose that God has predestined you to have.

Often, we hide and bury the truth deep down inside ourselves. Our truths are buried in our pains. When we come face to face with our pain, whether it is divorce, loss of a job, death of a relationship, or career aspirations, there are processes to find the strength in pain for it to become your power. Pain is always a symptom of something else that is coming from within that has not healed in your past or present situation. Your work is to discover what that variable is.

Authors Notes

A pain that came to me was when I had plans for my son's educational career. He decided not to go into his senior year in college, as this was not the path he desired. He often said this was mine and his dad's dream for him. Disappointed was an understatement. One morning during my quiet time of prayer and journaling, the Holy Spirit said to me, "He is my child, my plans, my kingdom." Now I don't know about you, but I often have some not so Christian moments with the Lord in our dialogue. He has made me flat foot sick of him on many occasions especially times when I did not ask for his direction nor opinion. To condense the story, I had to grieve the plans I had for my son. It was the death of the vision I had for ME, not my son. Allow me to give a quick back story on this child. When he was in the third grade, the church had an Easter egg hunt. My son had a great time and received an abundance of candy. A week later, I passed his bedroom door and noticed he had money all over his bed. I asked him where did he get the money from. He looked at me so innocently as he said, "I had a candy sale at school."

My response was, "Baby boy, where did you get the candy?" He told me about his process. My child took the candy from church and sold it to the kids at school. Lord, let me tell you I did not know whether to tap him or praise him for his business savvy. I tell this story because this has always been my son's temperament. He wanted to sell lemonade and chips when we would have garage sales. He would ask for this. My child has always been an entrepreneur. His father, grandmother, aunt, and I are all successful entrepreneurs. It is in his genes. Today he is walking, working, and trusting God in his own business. I grieved and believed, and I am good with it today. This is such a powerful feeling because I have assisted other women in not making the same mistake I did. When I see some of them, they thank me, especially the ones who escaped a lot of school debt. On a side note, it would be a blessing if he decided to finish college. But if not, I'm reminded— my child, my plans, my kingdom.

Reflection: What frightens, saddens, and hurts you? Establish this, these issues must be felt because this is the path to insight, power, and fulfillment.

> *"Remember you may plan your course, but the Lord determines your steps even through the pain. Breath and Grieve the pain, allow the Lord to turn it into Power, and trust the process. - Patricia Y. McCullough-Oliver*

<u>Payton</u>

Lady Von Kisser continued to deposit into Payton's life. Explaining she could not get to the point of even liking herself until a foundation within herself was built. Payton liked what she was saying and asked her how she did that. "By having a love affair with myself," Lady Von Kisser said again.

Von Kisser recalled a relationship that she was in when the individual started talking about what he did not like, the kind of people he did not like being around, the activities, lifestyles, or culture. It became clear to her that he did not like her because she represented all those dislikes. "You love me, but you don't like me," she said to this individual. At that point, she was set free. The fact that she would not conform to his world or the person he wanted her to become caused many issues in their relationship.

> *We as individuals must know who we are and who the Lord has predestined us to be. When we stay in that lane where others want us to, we are headed to destruction, depression, and detachment all wrapped into emotional abuse.* - *Patricia Y. McCullough-Oliver*

That was the beginning of the tear formation journey of Lady Von Kisser's life. She understood what was happening on the outside of her was because of what was going on inside. She removed herself from the toxic marriage never to entertain that relationship again. Before she left to go back to her cabin, Lady Von Kisser said, "Payton, if there is anything that you get from this life that you are running from, know this. Nothing physically touched the soul for the soul alone belongs to God and only He can fulfill those inner needs and desires. Not a man, nor possessions. So, my dear, I pray that you will learn some valuable things about yourself on this cruise and make conscious decisions and follow through with them. That will be the only way that you will be successful in your walk to self-love."

Payton took a deep breath as the waiter approached their table to see if they wanted dessert. While she looked down at her menu, there was a commotion happening outside on the deck that caused everyone to head outside. Payton looked up and turned around to see if she could see what was going on. When she turned back around Lady Von Kisser had left the table. The waiter said, "She asked me to tell you she retired for the evening and everything has been taken care of with dinner this evening."

Further Notes from the Author

Learning to first like yourself and believing you deserve to be in the best relationship, personally or professionally is easier said than done. I knew at a very young age what love looked like. When I saw women and their struggles within their relationships, I knew what it didn't look like. You must get to the point where you realize it's not your will but His will and allow the flesh to die to allow things to happen. Meaning, I had to make a conscious decision to work towards being the woman God had predestined me to be. When we are firmly established in our own inner love, everything is complete; this is the ultimate fulfillment, the ultimate contentment.

The first love affair one must have is a love affair with self. This process must start with an exercise that requires your participation. First, take inventory of yourself from head to toe. Make comments about what you like or dislike. For the attributes, you dislike, make a change if possible. For example, if you don't like your forehead, and there isn't anything you can surgically do; you must accept it. Please know acceptance does not necessarily mean liking. Once you have accepted everything about yourself, learn to appreciate you and all your goodness. When you love something, you do not allow others to misuse or abuse it. When you learn to have a love affair with yourself, you will no longer accept bad relationships from any area of your life. You must value yourself and know that you are worth everything. Do not settle for less! You must be ok on your own before you can be ok with someone else. Your perception of yourself must be based on truth and not your emotions or your reality. Until you value you and love you, you cannot have a healthy relationship. Think new thoughts about yourself. I journal and have done so for years. I write down the compliments that I have received through the years. It is just a reminder to me that I am "OK."

So true!

God- Control

You must have God control which makes room for self-control with your emotions. In Joyce Meyer's book *Living Beyond Your Feelings*, she says your emotions are like an undisciplined child. You must tell them what to do. We always tend to want to control and change someone else, but the only person you can control is yourself. This requires a decision and a process that may take time. Know when to step backward and allow others to find themselves. When someone must step back from the relationship with you, respect the decision, and keep it moving. Allow me to interject this: Sometimes they will come back just to see if you are still emotionally attached. Do *not* be a victim in Your Own Life. Again, love yourself and know that you deserve to be in the best relationships that add value to your life. As the expression goes, if you love something, let it go, and if it does not come back then it was not yours anyway. Let me add to this. Sometimes they come back, and they still are not for you. In the past, I did not give much credence to that statement. When I removed myself from relationships, many were great to me; they just were not necessarily good for me. Therefore, always be in God -control of emotional decisions.

Reflection: What is your truth? Please write down the truth about yourself, e.g., I am insecure; we live a lifestyle we cannot afford; I don't want to be in that organization. I do it just because of the influential members. My relationship is unfulfilling.

Author's Notes

Today, many people stay in relationships (personal and professional) for many wrong reasons, even when they know there is no happy ending. Marriages still exist today with knowledge of multiple affairs and multiple outside children. Most women come into relationships knowing that there are other women in the relationship. After they have decided to share, often they want to change the rules in the middle of the game. Many stay in these toxic relationships because of their partner's title or position. The game of pass the women around from friend to friend is still prevalent. People have friends who know their friends have unfaithful partners and stay quiet. Many women know these scenarios all too well because they are contributors. Your power is knowing what you are willing to put up with and work on the relationship. There are no perfect situations or people. As for the contributors in these scenarios, ask for forgiveness and start valuing yourself by implementing new transformational self-help skills. STOP DEVALUING YOURSELF.

TEAR-FORMATION

Payton

Payton had a restless night. Early that morning, she hoped to run into Lady Von Kisser before she left the ship. After the night with her listening to her journey, Payton reflected on her own life. She wanted to reach out to Lady Von Kisser during her stay there, but she had gotten away before she could get her cabin number.

When Payton stepped off the boat, there was such an awareness of nature in the air, it put her in a state of relaxation. It was surreal. While looking up in the sky, she noticed an open space, a space that allowed her to visualize what she wanted to become in life, especially after last night. It was a vision of freedom and awareness, which was something she had longed for but had no idea that she was missing. As she walked with her mind focused on the sky, she did not realize she was stepping down into a hole on her left side.

THE MIDNIGHT-CRY

Payton could feel herself falling, but something was stopping her. *Oh, my goodness,* she thought. A high pitch squeal made her step back. She looked down at a beautiful little white puppy.

"Where in the world did you come from?" she said.

A very petite young lady ran toward her." Me-Me! Oh, my Me-Me."

"Oh! I'm so sorry. I didn't see him." Payton had to say it a couple of times before the lady looked in her direction.

"It is *her,*" the woman said with a smirk and a glance.

"Excuse me, ma'am. I truly am sorry. I didn't see your dog," she continually tried to explain.

The lady picked up her dog and started walking to a bench across the street. Payton decided to follow her because she could see she was in some sort of state of mind. She acted as if Payton hadn't said anything to her. Payton observed the woman as she sat on the bench, rocking the dog, and looking out into space. The dog appeared ok. As Payton sat by them, the dog licked the woman's hands. It was such a strange encounter with this lady. She just sat there looking out over the water. What was interesting to Payton was she could feel this woman's sorrow as she looked out over the water with her.

Then the silence broke, and the lady spoke. "Today was supposed to be a great day. But today is a sad day."

Payton hesitated to say anything or ask any questions because she did not want to interrupt her train of thought. Payton sat there as the woman remained deep in thought.

"Tomorrow is not promised," she said repeatedly.

Silence again, this time for an exceptionally long time. Payton interjected, "Are you alright?"

Then something happened. A quiet weep came from her lips—a quiet whimper of pain. Not just some ordinary pain but that whimpering pain that gets stuck in your throat. Payton froze because she knew that pain. It is that pain when you hear or see something that has you in a place of SHOCK...a place that makes you numb. That place where you have an out-of-body experience. Like, is this me, is this my story. And better yet, how did I get here AGAIN?

Payton sat there because, from experience, she knew that there was not much anyone can do at this time but let them be. When you see people hurting, you must have a heart and a hand to relate to others' cries. A Heart to feel and a Hand to do.

Payton flinched when the dog jumped out of the lady's lap and ran out in the grass near the water, chasing after a beautiful red cardinal.

Before Payton was aware, she asked, "What happened?" And it just flowed. She started to tell her story.

She had just received THE call... the dreaded call. The call that every woman prays she will never receive. You sense that it's not a good call just by the vibe transmitted through the phone. "This is not working at this time in my life, I'm having a baby with someone else, or I'm moving on with someone else because I decided to take my life in a different direction." Or worse, they just stop calling and move on with their lives without a word to you. It's a feeling that starts in the pit of your stomach, then it moves up in your chest. You begin taking a deep breath, but as you exhale, the air will not come from your body. You can't move, you can't breathe anymore, your whole being is in shock. It's like your world just shut down. Your body just sits there, and then in some kind of way, a fake chuckle comes from your mouth out of nowhere. Your expression changes without any assistance from you. So, please believe, Payton knew all too well that feeling as the woman expressed herself. It is not like she hadn't been there on a couple of occasions before. Déjà vu all over again as she continued to listen. That cry, that MIDNIGHT cry you pray one day would stop flowing and stop hurting, but it continues until the tears run dry. One day it just stops, you try to move on, and you do, just move on. One day, you just move on. Before you know it, months and years have passed. Pain is what we feel when reality hits you in the face, heart, and gut. The woman talked about how she met, "the one," at least she thought he was the one. He never talked about marriage with her, but she assumed it would happen one day. He was everything that she thought she wanted; he was perfect, not perfect in the sense of perfection but perfect for her until he was not. She talked about how she had given her body to him, and the sad part was he was not that great in the intimacy department. She got caught up in having someone in her life. He filled the empty spaces in her heart that needed comforting. She had heard about his past, but she felt their relationship would be different. He would treat her differently because he said he had never met anyone like her. He made her feel special. It was the little things, the little gifts, the caring words of comfort. Out of all the women out there, he chose her. He was kind until he was not. While the pain was still raw, words came out that she felt like he should have been happy that she even wanted to be with him. She went on to say she had many others to select from also, but she chose to be with him, and he turns around and treats her in such a disrespectful manner. Everything was subjective from her experience. You could feel her hurt and anger, but most of all, you could see the physical scars, sores. Later there would-be scabs. The wounds of emotional pain.

> *Expectations are the mother of disappointments. Women tend to carry their emotions physically more than men. Women either put on additional weight or lose too much or become bitter or better. Either way, the wounds will show up later in life and other relationships; personally and professionally.* - *Patricia Y. McCullough-Oliver*

VALUE THE VAGINA

S uddenly, she stopped talking at Payton and started talking to her as she looked past her out to the open area.

"Young lady, answer me? Can you tell me where you can purchase a new vagina?"

Payton's eyes grew wide and she said, "Excuse me?"

"Let me rephrase it this way. Can you tell me *if* you can purchase a new vagina?" This time, the lady on the bench said it very slowly.

Payton was in shock and wanted to laugh at the same time. When Payton took the question a little more seriously, she looked at her and this time she did not want to laugh but had a bad feeling in her stomach.

"No, you cannot," said Payton.

"That is the correct answer," said the lady. "Then why do we let so many people test drive us and use us up? There are all kinds of procedures that we can have; we can tighten it up, etcetera, but it is still an old test-driven vagina," she said very slowly. "You see, missy when we allow any and everyone to deposit themselves into us, there is no value in that deposit or us. We are not receiving anything of value because they have been depositing themselves all over the world into others. It is free. If we start to wonder if he is in her, for example, maybe we will stop giving ourselves so freely just because something is making us feel a certain way. You see, I believe when we start being selective or better yet stop allowing anyone to deposit except our husband, we wouldn't make so many mistakes. Mistakes or bad decisions do not have to be fatal to be effective. You and I must start valuing our vagina." I know from this day on I will do just that.

As the woman continued to extend more wisdom, Payton thought about all the men she had allowed to test drive her through the years. Now she was not a loose woman with her morals, but she ashamedly counted her encounters. Whether it was three or twenty, there were too many allowed in the door to drive. What was left for her husband she had been praying for the Lord to bring her way? A car that so many had driven and have too many miles.

"Uhm." Payton shook her head.

Author's Note

Your body is priceless. In the Christian world, we have heard and read this statement as long as we have been introduced to Jesus. But for some, it is just a phrase. In our society, women give of themselves as if their bodies and vagina are worthless; this mindset baffles me. Stay with me on this one and let us not get offended by the word vagina. For those who are offended, the "official" word used in sex-ed classes, textbooks, and awkward conversations with the gynecologist is *pot*, with a long "o" (as in "note"); you use that word. Women use it like they are the only ones who possess one. They market it to get what they want and yet it's worthless because they put a street market value price on it and not the heaven market value. I still use the statement, "Can you tell me where you can purchase a new vagina?" for shock value because there are many procedures on the market now e.g., vaginal rejuvenation that restores your vaginal walls from pain and discomfort. There is the vaginoplasty that will tighten the muscles within the walls. But there will never be anything like the original function and feel that you were blessed with. You must value the vagina. If you do not, no one else will, and you will allow others to test drive you over and over again. Visualize this, when you have a hole that a screw must enter, there is a process to find the right screw to fit the right hole. You may continue putting the screw in the hole. You may continue taking it out over and over again. You may use a variety of screws of different sizes or colors looking for a screw that fits, or you just like how the screw looks in the hole, not having any purpose. During this process, you eventually strip the hole for the correct screw, meaning when you finally find the correct screw, or you are blessed with the correct screw, it no longer fits because it has been stripped. Now you will have to take the hole and get it worked on so there can be some support for the new screw that someone has blessed you with. I know that was a stretch, but you get the concept. Stop trying to fit all the wrong screws into your hole. Have you given your pot a name? Well, I ask because we seem to put a lot of value on names. We are quick to tell everyone the brand of our purse we carry, job titles, or relationships. Why? Because we associate it with some sort of value. Then why don't we value something as valuable as what the Lord has given us? When you give something a name, you give it ownership; you value it whether the connotation is negative or positive.

First of all, there is no perfect human being walking the earth. This is a fun topic in my workshops and speaking events. Value the Vagina is what I call it. I encourage women to value this part because it is the kingdom builder for real.

I ask the women what is her name? They look at me so funny. I ask what is your child's name? Often, they give that information to me without hesitation. You know that name because you value it. Why don't you value the product that assisted in the reproduction? The name of my personal pot is China. Why? Because, only the finest dining on my China—my husband.

Reflection: Give your pot a name that has valuable meaning. Treat it and cherish it by valuing it at the heaven market value.

<u>Payton</u>

As the dog ran back and jumped into the woman's lap, it caused her to take her focus off Payton and back on the dog because he continued barking at a red cardinal in the tree. Payton felt that was her cue to remove herself from the conversation. Besides, she felt she knew her walk better than anyone else, and she didn't need anyone to tell her how to live her life, especially with men. If anything, she had and was learning her lessons with all the men that she had experience in her life.

"The men in my life are the ones who are messed up. Look what they have lost. I'm a prize," she said as she walked away.

I get so tired of these women that have gone through something that feels that they are experts on relationships, she thought. *Besides that, the woman seemed like something was wrong with her. That man messed her up. Test drive me, please no one test drives me. I am doing the testing and driving.* This statement made her laugh. *Now that purchasing the vagina, that kind of got to me*, she thought as she walked away. *Oh well, anyway I need to continue to enjoy this day.*

The women on the bench did not even realize Payton walked away because she was so engulfed in pampering her dog. "I pray that will not be the final destination of my life—me and a dog. Lord, please do not let me become that woman," Payton said.

> *We must understand when dealing with others' pain; we must earn the right to speak into the lives of people's hearts about their mistakes, again a bad decision doesn't have to be fatal to be effective.*
> *- Patricia Y. McCullough-Oliver*

Mad Reflections

As Payton walked the streets, she reflected on the pain and shame of what she allowed herself to believe and experience in her last relationship. Was she just like the lady in the park just denying her very own personal experience?

There is never a day that goes by I don't think about the status of my love life. I'm sitting here in this city of love and romance, Italy. I see people walking around and holding each other's hands. But what is going on inside of them and their relationship? Are they with each other thinking about someone else's? Are they on this trip to work on the relationship? Hum, are they here without their mate or significant other? These thoughts sent a gut punch to her heart.

I wonder how many places my supposed man took his other women. At this point in Payton's life, everything was suspect.

"Here I was thinking I had an amazing relationship with the man of my dreams, but in reality, he was the man of my nightmare," she said to herself.

This made her mad all over again, knowing how wrong she was about this man that she thought was the one. The hardest part is when you try to replace that missing space in your heart that was once held by that person. She often cherished the fact that she made such good decisions, and now she looks back on her life and realizes she was also guilty of putting herself in a position for people to test drive her. She laughed for a short time again. That crazy woman made a lot of sense because she was getting used physically and emotionally. What would be left for her husband one day?

"How could he do that to me? Why? I cannot get that woman's statement out of my head," she said to herself.

As she continued to walk having her self-talks, she glanced at her side to see a couple walking hand in hand down the street. The first thing that came to her thoughts was, *I bet they are not married.* Now, why is that the case? Is this because married people do not act as if they love each other anymore? *Yes, that is exactly what I am saying. Not most anyway. I thought me taking this trip would make me stop thinking about him. But it has done no such thing.*

Author's Notes

What happens in relationships that make people search for others outside the relationships or not put as much time into them anymore? Why after a while we no longer feel desired anymore? These questions will be questions that will often have different responses based on whom you will ask because its subjective. Ask some men, and they will tell you it's just not in their nature to be with only one person. God knew this. Look at the New Testament at Solomon. If you ask a woman of a certain age they will say, "He should continue to love me no matter how I look or how long we have been together. So, I have gained a little weight." I used to think when men said, "She isn't the person that I married" it was such a terrible thing to say." I recall questioning a man, who made this statement. He said he recalls seeing someone he knew in his younger years, in fact, someone he had a crush on. The only way he knew that it was her is that he remembered the mole on her face. He said she even sounded different because when you gain excess weight, it changes your voice. His reason for the initial statement was, if he had married her, he would have been disappointed and strayed. This statement always interested me because when you look at some of the men, they were different looking at a younger age. I have caught myself saying this sometimes when I see men I knew and commented on how different they look now. The joke was always that someone dodged a bullet. Ok, we are never going to agree on some of these statements because I don't.

God is not going to allow a difficulty unless he is somehow going to use it for our good. Trust in me and I will use it for your good. The Apostle Paul said, "Put on the full armor of God (trust, peace, prayer, and faith)." Let me share with you something that sets me free.

Again, God handcrafts and is not a mass producer of his people. My walk will not look like your walk. Because you and I have been created by God as a unique person, his plan to grow you will not look the same as his plan to grow anyone else. What would grow a plant would starve a cow. Both need food, air, and water but in different amounts and conditions. A doctor cannot tell every patient who comes to see him with a different issue to take two pills and call me in the morning. Our children are all different. I don't love my children equally. I love them differently and uniquely. Growth comes with helping them based on their wiring. I know this firsthand because later in my life, the Lord blessed me with three bonus children. I have four different temperaments that I had to learn how to nurture and coach uniquely. Jesus knows what we need and how to get us there, especially through the trials and tribulations in life.

<u>Payton</u>

When Payton walked back to the ship and entered the hull, Lady Von Kisser came across Payton's spirit. With it being late, she decided to wait until tomorrow to reach out and share her experience with the lady and her dog. But, knowing she had an early departure to the city tomorrow, she wondered if she would have time at all to wait around and see her because after all, she does not have a cabin number.

Payton could hardly relax that night in her cabin because she was so excited about her next stop in the morning to Morocco. Her previous company's corporate office was there. Payton never had an opportunity to visit. This would have been her next business trip. She would have been coming to receive her sales award, but she was dismissed before this would happen. This was Payton's first time setting a record on the highest deal closed in the company in two years. *I'll make it a great day anyway,* she thought before falling to sleep.

ADDED VALUE

As she walked towards the building, she admired the massive structure. She pulled her camera out to take a picture of a large waterfall in front of the tall glass building. What a beautiful sight it was.

"Excuse me," a voice startled her.

It was a female in a beautiful red suit that exemplified power and confidence. She later learned her name was Sandy. The lady offered to take a picture for her which was a nice gesture. Payton detected an accent with an offside southern drawl.

"Oh, thanks. I would appreciate that very much," said Payton.

After the picture was taken, Payton and the young woman continued to converse. Payton later learned the woman was a C level executive who worked for her company for over eighteen years. She also learned that the woman was remarkably successful in her career. She started in the position of executive secretary and climbed the corporate ladder. Currently, she was Vice President of Marketing. As Payton listened to her story, she was surprisingly enlightened on what leadership was not. She told Payton, "People did not want to be managed, they wanted to be led. A good leader says, 'let's do this together' and not 'go get it done.'"

She continued with her personal story. "My job advanced into a career when I learned how to be an added value person to my employees and then my company. I developed into caring more about the people than I did about the position, and let me tell you, my employees worked hard for me and the company. Before I could feed my people I had to learn to lead my people. Again, I elevated instead of stagnated.' I was always willing to listen and learn even from the staff that I led. They needed to know that they were valued and heard. I volunteered, and I helped as many people along the way as I could. I watched my tone with people and always communicated with respect. I spoke and smiled all the time, even when they were doing things that were of no value. I kept this disposition even when my body nor mind felt up to the task. I always asked others how they and their family members were doing, and left thank you and job well done notes on their desk occasionally. Conversely, I left support notes when they were struggling in productivity. People will give you their hand when you show them your heart," said

Sandy. She went on to say that we have to be a leader in your spirit not in your flesh.

Payton realized her whole career looked nothing like the characteristics Sandy shared with her. She realized how selfish she had been as an employee to her team. Most of all, she became aware of some hard-cold facts. She was not a leader; in fact, she exemplified everything a leader was not. Payton saw that so much of her personality flaws were her covering up what she did not want others to see: insecurity and selfishness. Her true self. As she stood there reflecting, she realized something major was missing within her. This explained why she was not living a conscious life that impacted her career. All she could do was stand there and look at the building and the beautiful red cardinal on the tree.

> *As a leader, remember to lead by serving and serve by leading. Also, your job is what you are paid to do. Your call is what you are made to do.* - *Patricia Y. McCullough-Oliver*

Author's Notes

As I worked on this book, I realized that I have always been an added value person. I always want people to be ok. Early on in my life, it was to my detriment because I had the "disease to please." When the added value concept becomes off-balance, it will cause problems and sadly, heartbreak. It's not because of what someone did to you, but what you did to yourself.

People will do three things to you; they will add, subtract, or divide. Often, not necessarily people, but you and your actions will add to this equation. Payton had to learn this the hard way by losing her job and traveling across the world to find out she had a lot of character flaws that were the consequence of her being removed from her position in the company and others' lives.

Reflection: Are you an adder, subtractor, or a divider in others' lives?

I was a pleaser, and may I add, queen pleaser. I wanted everyone to like me. Now that is not a bad characteristic unless it undervalues you and what you bring to relationships, both personal and professional. For me, it becomes a bad thing when you stop loving yourself and instead take care of others' needs ahead of yourself too often.

THE CONVERSATIONS

Payton

There are times in our lives that we just cannot understand what is going on, and then there are times when we *really,* do not know what is going on.

As Payton continued to walk this path of self -discovery, she often wondered what was ahead of her. "When Lord? When?" was a statement she had been making most of her life.

When will my life be what I want it to be and what I deserve it to be? Lord? WHEN! I know I have been living a good life, but I want to live a great life. I keep reading and hearing about so many other people's lives on and off the television. I am just not satisfied; I want more, I need more. I know, after I get more, I will be better. I just know this within my heart. I can feel it. I need to feel it; she continued to speak within herself. What Payton was realizing is that things were just not lining up in her life the way she planned.

On this morning, Payton was not even sure what the next stop was on this trip. She was a little drained after yesterday's encounter with the lady at her old corporate office. The loudspeaker on the ship announced that they were at their next destination, and she got off the ship and on the tour bus. The tour bus stopped to allow them to view the city. As she walked, she noticed this beautiful park across the street from where the bus dropped them off. Suddenly, a peaceful feeling entered her spirit. The breeze caressed her face. When she focused on the beauty of the park, she noticed a couple. The couple sat on the bench and the woman rubbed the back of the guy's neck. This gesture touched Payton's heart first and then her eyes because this was how she communicated affection in her previous relationships. As the couple talked, Payton noticed the woman was deep into the conversation and emotionally connected, but she could not see that connection from the guy. His body language showed he was not connected to the conversation. Most of her companions were emotionally disconnected; this is how she knew the body language so well. Payton's mind went back to her past thinking about why she continued to deal with her relationships. It was because being by herself was not an option. Payton stayed until they decided they wanted to move on; she never made the first move. Most of her men felt that all women wanted the same thing: material things. This was not just an image she saw with this couple, but her story. At the time she had no idea how much of it was like her story. As she looked at them, she wondered what their story was really like. You know that saying, "Things were not always like what they look like." But deep down in her spirit, she wanted to know their story. Something was telling her that there was much more there than meets the eye. When you have lived that lie, you can smell it a mile away. Payton could smell the LIE. So, she moved forward in that direction to do a little investigating.

She took the bench right next to them, but she made sure there were a couple of spaces in between. Payton was glad that she had her shades in her side pocket. She put them on and relaxed her body on the bench. As the tiredness entered her body, she realized how tired she was from the ship and bus ride earlier. Payton decided to skip the next stop of the tour that the cruise was giving because the next words she heard from the couple got her attention. She slumped down on her bench in a more comfortable position.

"What do you mean perfect us, imperfect me?" The female voice rose above the sounds of the tourists.

Oh, those words, this is not good, Payton said to herself. Oh, Lord, is this River again, she thought.

"Like I said, what do you mean perfect us imperfect me? You are telling me that all this time?," the girl said.

A loud horn went off, and Payton could not hear the next part of the conversation.

"Dang," Payton said. She was a little louder than she expected, so she clamped her hand over her mouth. She found herself smirking because she knew she was wrong for trying to eavesdrop on the couple. You could tell the conversation was getting a little heated by the way the female perched on the front edge of the bench and the way the guy sat back as if he was not trying to hear all that she was saying.

"Do you mean after all this time; this is where we are now? Say something, say something," she continued to say.

It was obvious he was not engaging in any dialogue for her to continue repeating those words. Then Payton sensed something—the quietness, and then there it was. She could hear the tears before she could see them.

"I have given so much—" a siren washed out her words again.

When Payton turned her head to see what the commotion was with the siren, she did not see the guy get up and leave. Payton turned to get back in position to listen to the conversation, but the couple was gone; he was gone physically, and it was obvious she was gone emotionally. The woman sat there as if lost and in shock. Again, another look that Payton was familiar with.

Payton did not know what to do, and as she finished her last thought, the woman said, "Well, I guess you heard all of that."

This caught Payton off guard because she had to look around to see who was talking and who they were talking to. The woman turned her head in Payton's direction and said, "I'm talking to you. You have to be deaf to not have overheard our conversation."

Payton tried to take it all in. "Well ahh yes. I did kind of hear a little of the conversation at least your part."

The woman gave Payton a stern look like she wanted to say something mean, but it passed through her. While Payton looked at her in the eye, both had different expressions on their faces. Payton's look was that of surprise and the woman was that of pain. Suddenly, the tears came streaming down her cheeks, and the women put her head in her hands and wept louder. *Oh my God,* Payton said to herself.

"Oh, I am so sorry." Payton realized the woman could not hear her because she was sobbing so loudly. Payton knew the cry so well. It was that midnight cry that so many have experienced in their lives at one time or another. Payton thought *I am seeing many of these cries on this trip. Lord, what is going on with these women?*

"I'm so sorry," Payton said, as she walked over to the women's bench. Payton moved with caution because she did not want this woman to haul off and hit her for invading her privacy. Payton had no problem with defending herself; she had a lot of experience in that arena from her past. Her PR statement has always been "Don't let this image fool you. I will cut you." Payton decided it would be safe to just sit there and let her finish crying and allow her to speak when she wanted or needed to. Her objective was just to be there. Payton had learned this in her earlier years of sales training. Mirror your client. Payton turned her head to observe how green and beautiful the grass was and how peaceful her surroundings were. As she took in her surroundings, she saw a red cardinal. "You guys are following me," she said and laughed.

"How did I get here again?" the lady said. Quicker than she realized, Payton swung her head around when she heard those familiar words.

Payton said, "I wish I had the answer to that million-dollar question. I have said those exact words too many times in my life."

Both women just looked at each other, paused, and then turned their heads away from each other. They looked forward while continuing to stare out in the street.

Slowly, the woman started to speak. "I thought we were in a relationship, only for him to tell me we were just in a friendship." She still stared towards the street.

Payton swallowed and said, "May I ask how long you were in the relationship? I mean friendship?"

"Three years off and on."

Payton's eyes grew wide. "Excuse me," came out of Payton's mouth before she could catch the words.

The woman faced Payton with a sad and embarrassing smirk. Tears smeared black mascara around her eyes. "Yes, three years, but we were just friends," she said sarcastically. "I gave more to this relationship than any others. I just knew this was my husband. I just knew it. I felt the physical and emotional things that I had never experienced before."

"That's where you made your mistake," a voice said, seemingly out of nowhere.

The two women jumped with a scream and started looking around. The voice came from behind the bench. A woman behind the bench was stretching as she looked up from the ground at them. She laughed. "I'm sorry, but I didn't mean to interrupt your conversation while you were talking."

"Who are you and how long have you been down there?" Payton and the woman said in unison, "Oh, quite a while. I was here before you and your boyfriend, I mean you and your friend sat on this bench." Amusement etched itself across her face. "I was going to get up and leave, but something told me to stay. I was not trying to listen, but you guys were talking very loudly, and besides, I was here first."

The woman on the bench looked at Payton and the new woman. "This day is turning out to be a day of all days. Two women I do not even know, know more about my business than my closest friends. I keep people out of my personal business."

"Umm, is it because you did not want them to know the true relationship?" Payton asked.

The women on the bench became a little perturbed.

"Listen, ladies, you don't know me, and I don't know you," said the lady on the ground in her colorful warmups. "But I do know a little something about relationships."

What are you, some kind of psychologists?" said the lady sitting on the bench.

The woman on the ground said, "As a matter of fact, I am. But I'm more than just a psychologist. I have walked this walk and through that phrase myself. How did I get here again? I was the queen of saying that statement because I have said that in more than one relationship until I understood my position."

"Your position!" Payton and the women said in unison again and looked at each other and laughed.

The woman on the ground smiled and said, "Yes, my position."

Now I pray this woman is not getting ready to talk to me about no sexual positions, Payton thought.

Your Position

The women decided to take the conversation inside, so they walked to a coffee shop in the area. It occurred to Payton she had no idea what their names were. A sense of oneness came over her, as if they had some unspoken kinship and experience in relationships, especially for them to have recited that mantra: "How did I get here again?"

The women found a location to sit and talk. Payton was not sure how this coffee talk would turn out, but she was ok with trying to listen to this woman who claimed to know about relationships. *I just really want to see what she is talking about with this position mess*, Payton thought.

Payton later learned the psychologist's name was Dr. Tira Collins originally from Port Moody, Canada. "What would you think if you saw a little child at the age of five trying to drive a car and the parents were in the back seat?" asked Dr. Collins.

"I would think that is careless and dangerous," said the woman.

"Yes," said Dr. Collins, "because she was in the wrong position in the car. Think about that concept in relationships. When you are out of your rightful position, especially in the position that God didn't ordain you to be, then things are out of order."

"I have and always will be a hopeless romantic, the happy ever after girl, that is me. So, when a male friend Rev. Arthur introduced this relationship concept to me, I started implementing it and it saved me a lot of heartache in my life. Just as we learn life skills in other areas of our lives, I suggest we implement them in our relationships," Dr. Collins went on to explain. "There are a lot of dimensions in relationships, whether personal or professional e.g., promotions and demotions. These actions occur many times without our permission. You may think you are in a committed relationship because you have been identified as a friend or companion, but you're not. Worst of all, you are either just something to do for the time being or on the shelf relationship, just killing time until something better comes along. Nothing is wrong with any of these positions if there is a mutual understanding and agreement. The problem is when there is no communication; frustration, disappointment, and hurt show up. I have seen this scenario in relationships played out too many times. Both of you may have experienced this at one time or another in your life."

Both women stayed quiet as their thoughts took them to some unhappy times in their past. Dr. Collins gave an example:

> Boy meets girl, boy likes girl. Girl likes boy a great deal, boy and girl proceed to develop friendship, sex jumps in, girl thinks committed relationship, the boy thinks just friends. Boy meets a new girl, boy dates a new girl. The old girl sees the old boy with the new girl. Old girl feels hurt, disrespected, and played on. Nope, says the boy. I never told you that you were MY girl. The old girl says, "BUT you, you, YOU, You, You..."

Relationship Stages

Author's Notes

a. **Friendship***:* A healthy friendship is one of communication that time and distance cannot destroy; a friendly relation or intimacy; NOT INTERESTED IN ANYTHING EMOTIONAL but can have sexual activity not COMMITTED LOVE. Acquaintance and sexual relationship (s)

b. **Companionship:** Companionship can be platonic or romantic. Companionship refers to the company, friendship, or the state of being with someone in a friendly way; WILL DATE OTHERS. Open sexual relationship (s)

c. **Relationship**: A connection, existing between people related to or having dealings with each other.

Two individuals deciding on a committed connection involves the two people in the relationship; I WILL DATE ONLY YOU.

The value in these stages is understanding your position. In any of these relationships, you can have your definition. Just make sure you both understand the truth and ask for a nod of confirmation that our interpretation of the definition is the same. What this does is allow fairness on your part and keeps your character, emotions, and body intact.

Also, be aware that once the relationship has been established and a commitment is made, there is still room for dishonesty, disappointment, and frustration. Feelings and emotions sometimes have a life of its own; therefore, individuals may confess to be on one level and still misrepresent.

The truth to this all is that individuals are often hurt because they have no idea where they stand in the relationship. Ask questions; re-evaluate the situation often to see where you stand e.g. what level you are on. Remember, relationships can change without your permission. Knowing your position can help ease a lot of pain and misunderstandings.

Let me give you another example of the importance of the position. Fire is helpful, and it is hurtful. The same item in different positions yields different outcomes. We need fire to eat and keep us warm, but the fire that is placed in the wrong location and out of control destroys. The same thing occurs in relationships when you know your position, your chances of being hurt or hurting someone else are minimal.

In my marriage, my husband and I make it a point to monitor often. Ask questions continuously. Is our commitment the same? Does more attention need to be put into a certain area of the relationship? Again, ask questions and re-evaluate often. I made it my mission in my dating days to ask, "What do you want and expect from me?" when I saw the friendship was growing. I think that is a direct question worthy of a direct answer. I do this because it sets boundaries. If they want something that I can't give, let's keep it moving, this way we are not wasting each other's time. If you don't have anything emotionally or physically to give to the relationship, at that time in your life, make them aware of your emotional place. If they need some emotional fulfillment, then you can't be that person. You can't give what we don't have. Allow me to explain continued Dr. Collins.

Toxic Relationships

Some relationships are good *for* you but not good *to* you. Or some relationships are good *to* you but not good *for* you. You could be at a great job e.g., salary and benefits, but you and your boss's relationship is toxic with no room for growth in the company. You may be in a relationship where you like everything that it has to offer e.g., lifestyle, but the person is not good to you e.g., emotional and physical abuse. There are people with different mindsets that allow them to stay in toxic relationships. I like to call them the Rider, and the Floater. One stays too long, and the other does not stay long enough. The Rider has the ride and die personalities that will hang in there through thick or thin. It's an unconditional love behavior that lives close to a danger zone and passes all understanding. They will forgive until they can forgive no longer. The problem with this behavior is most of the time, they do not know when to get off. They will stay with all the abuse, emotional or physical. The company has promoted people over you for the fifth time. The family member has abused your kindness for years. The marriage has birthed the ninth outside child. Ok, I may be adding on a bit much, but you get the picture. They never know when to say enough is enough. This is why learning to have a love affair with yourself will not allow someone to put you in a Rider position any longer than your conscience desires. Floaters, all they do is float; they do not commit to anyone or anything. When the relationships have a hint of being uncomfortable, they are gone because they are afraid of commitments. This character trait carries over into the workforce and is quite common in the religious arena. For instance, if the minister does something they do not like, they're on to the next church. We called them church hoppers because they move from congregations repeatedly until they find one that will allow them to be comfortable with their behavior. Toxic people will never change until they have reason to change. Often if they change for the wrong reason, they will just change victims. Be aware. Les Brown said every year he works on getting toxic people out of his life. We should apply that concept often. The Lord is telling you to remove people and then there are ones who are supposed to remain in your life because they may be your assignment or your ministry, I like to say.

Reflection: Allow the Lord to reveal who you need to remove and who should stay. Just make sure the Lord has advised you to remove them. Some may be there for your spiritual growth and theirs also.

Author's Notes

Why is it that some individuals can move on from relationships with a little more ease than others? Allow me to tell you how. I have often been asked how I can end relationships and move on and continue with a friendship with the individual. My answer is often, I decided the relationship was not giving me a good return on my investment, and the investment was my time, energy, etc. I value myself, and I know what I bring to the table. I loved myself more than the variables in the relationship. I can continue the relationship in a friendly manner because I'm no longer emotionally connected to them in the same manner. I looked at the spirit or strongholds controlling their actions. I separate the action from the person. I'm fully aware I can't always control the circumstances of my relationships but I can always control my own, thoughts of how I handle the relationships.

There is no perfect vessel walking this earth. Some just take longer to mature, and I know that I can't change anyone, so I don't try. I say to myself that it is not my ministry to save but the Lord's. My goal most of the time is to make sure I have deposited something in the relationship that they will always remember and grow from. I have made some men good husbands for other women. I have always known I was a seed planter. My major objective is to make sure I'm adding to others' lives and not subtracting. Leaving a lasting good impression meant that I grew from the relationship also. Staying excited when relationships ended helped me also because I know that the Lord has something in store for me that will be much better. When things don't turn out the way I have prayed and believed, my next statement is always, "Ok Lord, if that was not it, I can wait until you bring the next opportunity, person, client, etc." I believe you attract what you project. The Law Attraction means that I stay positive, upbeat, uplifting, and continue to project my nurturing and funny personality.

Payton

As Payton watched and engaged in the conversation something happened. Payton stopped listening and started hearing. There is a difference.

Dr. Collins decided to give them both something for free. "In my practice, there are many things that I have learned from my clients. I can recall someone I met at one of my Conferences. Her name was Patricia McCullough -Oliver. She was an award-winning author who wrote a book called *Your First Love Affair with Self.* We sat down and talked, and she shared this valuable information about a love affair with self. I started incorporating them into my sessions."

This got the ladies' attention but most of all Payton. This love affair stuff was coming up again. Lady Von Kisser talked about this.

"Payton, Payton," Dr. Collins said.

Payton came out of her trance. "Yes, yes. I am sorry my mind went somewhere else. Please go on. I am interested in hearing more."

"Let me get to the point," said Dr. Collins, "I will give the CliffsNotes version. Having a love affair with yourself must start with yourself. You must take a visual individual assessment of yourself. You must commit to being honest, I mean as honest as you have ever been. To do this, you must start from a place of truth. Your truth. Step one, position yourself in front of a mirror and evaluate your whole body from the top to bottom. Say yes to body parts that you like and no to body parts that you do not. If there is something you can do about what you don't like, then make the change. If there is something you don't like but can't change, then accept it and move on." It is a decision, accept it and move on.

Payton took mental notes. "Now ladies, the key to this self-examination is that acceptance has nothing to do with liking. Take me for example. I am a small-breasted person;

therefore, when I realized that I was not going to get breast enhancement, I learned to accept my body type and breast size. Let me tell you this. I walk like I am a DD. When I share this at my conference, many get a big laugh out of it. I can go into more detail, but that is the first step to liking the real you. You must like yourself before you can learn to love yourself."

The day was getting late. They decided to go their separate ways and were advised to get the book. It will give you a plan to get to your goal. It is called Your *First Love Affair with Self* by Patricia Y. McCullough-Oliver.

Reflection: What did you find out about yourself reading information on position, toxic relationships, and the statement that you can't give what you don't have?

Third Chance

Payton

Payton was exhausted the next day because of the long day in the park with Dr. Collins. All the new information she had received the previous days overwhelmed her. On this day, she decided to take some time for herself, by herself to focus on her needs. This was a new space for her because most of her life she was a people pleaser. At this juncture of her life, she did not have the strength nor the desire to seek to please anymore. Then, suddenly, this feeling came over her: forgiveness. That word nor the feeling that came with it would not go away. How many people had been removed from her life by her?

Payton started counting. When she first started going through this separation phase of her life, it felt so wonderful not having to deal with individuals who no longer added value to her life. She felt that same feeling as she thought about it. But as of late, she started feeling a sense of loneliness and a feeling of self-examination. She said to herself, *I never thought about how many people put me out of their lives or how many people had their spirit tell them to remove me from theirs.* OMG, it was at this moment, Payton did the list, no, not the list of how many partners you have had in your life, the list of how many people she had removed from her life. Her thought process took her back to people who she did not have the same type of relationships with people who just were not there anymore. This was not the first time she looked at herself and examined how she treated people or the way she spoke about people. If there is one thing Payton knew about herself it was that she had the gift to gab. Never was she the type of person who maliciously said hateful things about people. Most of the time, she spoke her truth. People sometimes say, "I was speaking my truth," but most of the time it's about someone else. You could not possibly know someone else's truth unless you lived within their souls. Then the Holy Spirit revealed the truth to her, and she stopped instantly in her footsteps. So, on this day she was supposed to be spending time with herself, she was spending time examining herself.

Often, we think we are doing something good by removing others out of our life. If you are not evaluating your experience, there is a possibility there is no movement or growth. Let's not look at activity as accomplishments. Why, because maybe the Lord had you in their lives as your ministry for your spiritual growth. Again, make sure you seek the Lord if these individuals should no longer be a part of your life. Misery or ministry, that is the question.
Patricia Y. McCullough-Oliver

Payton had girlfriends who were there for her during some very tough times in her life. When she needed money, a shoulder to cry on, or simply a good old hug, they were there. Then she recalled a situation with one of her dear girl-friends who put her out of her life. Now, this was a friend who she did not need to talk to every day, but when they got together, it was like old times. This friend got into a relationship that disappointed Payton. Her disappointment came from the fact that her friend was doing the same thing to another woman her ex-husband did to her, cheating and doing things in public with other women while they were still together. Of course, Payton spoke her truth, but the problem was she was speaking that truth to someone else and it got back to her friend. When she thought about this, how could she have discussed that situation with someone else other than her friend? She thought about how many others are guilty of this, not having empathy for the people we call friends. She often thought about friends in her life who were no longer there, and she realized there is one common denominator and that was her. How many friends had she hurt in her life saying things that she didn't mean? She prayed on occasions that the Lord would restore some relationships and others she was ok that they were now just acquaintances.

Well, once Payton reflected over this, she realized that in some relationship, we are given a chance and then a second chance. As this revelation hit her spirit, she wished some of her past friends would give her a THIRD CHANCE and herself the same.

> *Friends may not be all that you want them to be, but God made them be all they need to be in your life. Which will leave room for the next friend that you may be their new assignment. Commit forgiveness and submit.* – Patricia Y. McCullough-Oliver

Author's Notes

I recall me thanking the Lord for the many toxic people who were no longer in my life, but during this particular fast 2010, the Holy Spirit said to me, "Have you ever thought I was removing you from other people's lives?" Man, that hit hard. Most of the time we think more of ourselves than we are. Roman 12:3 says, "For by the grace given me I say to every one of you: Do not think of yourself more highly than you ought to." The Lord revealed so much to me about myself. He let me know that every season of my life was divine separation intervention. Every person, every disappointment is the process of God developing me into the person I am today.

Is this something that you would have liked if the opportunity presented itself? A THIRD CHANCE, for me, I came to realize that sometimes there are things that I missed from the old friendships. There were some great times and things of value that I cherished in the relationship. I know there are some friendships that I have prayed for the Lord to heal and restore. I will walk in faith and believe that he will do so in his time if it is his will. I used my personal scale to determine whether I was going to put in the effort to restore the friendship before I wrote them off. Are their friends worth fighting for? If they were, I went back and tried to work it out. If there was not enough value in the friendship to keep it, I just kept it moving and allowed the friendship to be what it was. I challenge you to do the same. Make a list of all the people who YOU removed out of your life and not necessarily the Lord. Pray over the names and step away. You will be surprised at the names you are given to fight for. When I did this, I realized some people are in our lives as a part of our ministry. Also, understand the relationship you go back and fight for may never be the same. The Lord forgives us, but there is still a consequence associated with our actions. There are many people behind prison walls that have repented and found Christ for the first time. But there is still a consequence for the decisions that got them there in the first place. I want to give you a nugget. What if we try a new approach? What if we tried to look at our friends from a different lens? What if we changed places with them and pretended, they were us? This process will put us in a different mindset. I found out through my different transformations in life, the Isolation period to be exact. I had a different mindset going through the many changes in my life. I was not my usual self. What if we forgave our friends? What if we went back to them and told them what we thought about them at that phase in our lives? What Payton would have realized was there was something deeper going on within her. Payton realized she was saying hurtful things about a friend because she was mad and disappointed at her friend for doing something to another woman, hurting her when she went through the same thing in her marriage. Payton realized her relationship with her friend would have been different had she just talked to her instead of others. Deep down, she wished that some of her friends would have given her a THIRD CHANCE.

Friendships are important. I realized that I was not a good friend in my friendships. I never really nurtured my friendships as much as I would have liked. When things were going on within, I would disconnect from my friends. Many did not know the reason for the disconnect was me needing to get in tune with my spirit. When situations came up, all I wanted to do was connect with my spirit and hear from the Lord. I just wish I could have handled my disconnects differently with my friends. I wish I could have just said, "I need some time to myself," instead of just disappearing within myself. If I had the maturity in my life at that time, I think transitions and transactions would have been different. We should look at our friendships as liquids and solids—allowing them to move with the transformations of our friends. That is not always the case with our friendships. We are such creatures of habit that we sometimes never try to see things from other points of view. Some people will never be our friends. Have you ever been friends with someone, they became friends with a mutual friend, but when you go back to the relationship, things have changed with the mutual friend? That can happen. Again, if the relationship is worth saving, do more investigating. How about reflecting on your true relationship and determine whether what you heard about them sounds like something they would do or say, investigate the situations. Let's give others the THIRD CHANCE.

> ***Stop expecting others to meet the needs that only God can meet in our friendships.***
> – *Patricia Y. McCullough-Oliver*

The Victim

Payton

Payton didn't sleep well on this particular night aboard the ship. She wasn't sure if it had to do with it being the last leg of the cruise while she still had so much turbulence in her soul.

Sure, she had met some interesting people who instilled some wisdom on knowing she was a child of God, learned how to have a love affair with herself as Lady Von Kisser shared, and understanding position, added value, and third chances, but there was still something missing.

Getting away on this cruise spending time with herself turned out to be challenging. Payton was a lost and broken soul who had no idea she was lost. She knew she was seeking something, but what she was seeking, she had no idea. As Payton walked across the streets in a city that she often dreamed of visiting, her heart reminisced about the many relationships she had in the past, many wonderful and not so wonderful ones: doctors, lawyers, ambassadors, politicians, athletes. That hurt from her relationships, both personal and professional had left such bitterness in her. Payton still felt as if she did not know the whys and all the dysfunctions in her life.

Author's Notes

Have you ever asked yourself how in the world you wound up in some of the relationships or situations you found yourself in, whether they were personal or professional? How did it just happen to me? The truth is it didn't just happen. You *allowed* it to happen, maybe I need to qualify that – not all people or circumstances. Many individuals often play the blame game and have a victim mentality. At some point in your life, you have to become accountable for your actions.

Relationships require discipline in your thoughts that help with your emotions; no one can map out your relationship for you except for you with the guidance of the Lord. We must experience personal change before we can implement public change. Your relationship with God will shape your perspective of how you operate within your relationships.

> *Your choice starts with your thoughts, your thoughts become your words, your words become your actions. Each day decide to have life-giving thoughts.* - *Patricia Y. McCullough-Oliver*

Reflection: Give me one sit down and tell me briefly about your relationship history, and I will tell you about you and what is going on inside. Again, Expectations are the mother of dissapointments. What are your relationships saying about you?

Write down five current or past relationships and identify the behavior or characteristic with an adjective. Watch for a pattern.(Ex). Fred / emotional abusive

THE DUKE

Payton

S oon, Payton will discover life will never appear to be the same on this final day of her travels. As she prepared for her day, she decided her first stop would be a quick workout and then breakfast. As she headed toward the hull of the boat to the upper deck and looked out over the ocean, she noticed how gloomy the day was. It was not as beautiful as it had been. Much of the fog lingered over the water, and it reminded her of how she felt within: full of emotional fog, seeing nothing, feeling nothing. *Umm, ok Lord what do I do now. I have come all this way and even though I heard many perspectives of love and relationships. I have tried to comprehend but I still feel the same way I felt starting this journey,* Payton thought.

Many times, in life through our spiritual journey, it's not what is happening on the outside of us but what is happening on the inside. The Lord is interested in what He is doing through us and not to us. Our bodies and minds are continually being formed by what is going into them. We must always trust the process of what is happening in our lives. - Patricia Y. McCullough-Oliver

This was becoming unpleasant to Payton because she was hoping to feel something after all the money and time she spent on this cruise. Standing there, her appetite and her desire to workout had passed. She shook her head and rebuked that unhealthy friend because she did not want to do anything most of the time. Her name was Procrastination. *Not today my sister, I am moving today because this is my last day here on my supposed to be self-discovery trip,* she thought. She laughed because this was the first time, she expressed a name for the cruise. After all, at first, it was just to spend some money to make her feel better from the pain of cheating River. Payton went to her room to change and started her way off the ship. She was unsure where she was headed because she did not sign up for a tour, but she was headed somewhere. The fog was lifting; she could see little peeks of the sun coming out. A nice breeze made the day bearable and not as hot as the previous days. It was quiet in this city. Not many people were out, but there were many horses out and about. Payton had no idea where she was. She had gotten off of the ship with no plan. She smiled a little because this behavior had become a common activity. She hadn't even noticed all the stops that were included in this cruise. She just blindly accepted what the travel agent gave her since it was on such short notice. All she was interested in was getting away. So today was no different. As she continued to walk, she saw a path leading down a long trail full of trees, no water this time, just trees. It had a very solemn look to it. The trees were not pretty, but there was something mystical about this spot. Although it was a little scary, her spirit was drawn to it. As she walked the trail, it got thinner and thinner. She decided to turn back a couple of times, but she had this urge to continue down the path. Just when she thought she couldn't go any further, something amazing appeared.

"Oh," Payton said as her eyes opened wide. One of the most beautiful homes she had ever seen in her life came into view. It was so large she couldn't see where it stopped or where it began. The land was massive; the waterfalls shot so high in the air; she couldn't see where they stopped. There was no fog on this side of the property. Payton stood there and took it all in. She closed her eyes to not only see but to feel the presence of this place. A wonderful breeze blew her hair slightly over her face. The aroma of flowers and grass was so vivid to her eyes and nose. As she looked around, there was a stoop to her right, so she knew this was someone's property. But she was not ready to leave, at least not right now. So, she sat and closed her eyes to bask in the home's presence. Suddenly, the leaves moved as if someone walked her way. She quickly opened her eyes and jumped up.

"Oh, I'm sorry." She started rambling off to this strange man who stood there saying nothing. She waited for him to say something to her, but he never did. He just looked at her strangely.

"Sir, hello," Payton said.

He still said nothing. As he looked at her, he gestured with his head to follow him. Payton hesitated for just a second, but she was intrigued to see what lay on the other side of this massive place, and besides, for some reason, there was no fear in her spirit. Payton was always a very adventurous young girl, and nothing had changed at this period in her life. As she followed him at a distance, looking all around her, she noticed that his pace slowed down as if they were approaching something or someone. Soon after, she saw it was a person. A man, or should she say the presence of something out of a fairy tale. At first, all she could see was the back of him, but as he turned around, words could not explain his stature. It was not the handsome look, although he was something stunning, his presence was so surreal, powerful, and distinguished. He looked like someone from the 18th century; a quiet giant came to her thoughts. He looked at her, and this time she opened her mouth quickly because she did not know what his next actions would be, after all, she was trespassing on this property.

"Sir, I just want to say—"

"No need to explain, my dear. I was expecting you."

Now, this threw her for a loop. "Expecting me?"

"Yes." He smiled and spoke in a deep and mystical voice. "Very few people stumble onto my property. The entrance is designed to keep intruders away with its haunting look, and for those who continue all the way through, it is usually someone I am intrigued to meet. Besides, nothing gets past my angels—" He looked at the other man. "I mean my groundsman," he said quickly.

Oh! He must be a deeply religious man to say his angels, she thought.

"I could see you were simply curious. So again, I was expecting you."

This time his words were a little more inviting.

"Please come and walk with me. My name is Sir Duke Lennard. "Please follow me. You were intruding on my daily walk around the grounds, but you may join me if you wish."

"I would love to. I mean yes, I would like to join you on your walk."

Payton made small talk about how beautiful his property was and her travel on the cruise ship that caused her to stumble upon his property.

"Ms. Payton, do you believe in divine interventions?"

"I guess I do," said Payton. "I have heard people talk about that happening in their lives but not me. Each time I met a man, I thought that was God intervening on my behalf, only to later find out it was my fleshy work." She gave a short laugh to shake off the embarrassing statement she made. She could not recall if she had ever said that out loud and now that she had, it made her feel small.

He smiled along with her. "Young lady, you are not by yourself. It is just fate that we are nurtured to believe in our true existence on the earth."

Although Payton was not sure she agreed, she still said ok. As they continued to walk, they came upon this statue in the area of this property. He stopped and looked at it with such passion. Payton stood there with him and observed how he admired the hunk of clay with a beautiful cardinal sitting on her shoulder. The statue had no face, no nothing, but it had a presence and an apparent impact on his life. She could tell it was a female just by the way his eyes lit up, and then there was a strange sadness that appeared just as fast as the happiness. It was a sadness and a stare she had seen before somewhere else; she just could not put her finger on it.

I wonder what that is about, Payton thought.

"Mrs. Payton?"

She smiled and said, "Miss Payton"

"Miss Payton it is. You are a very intriguing young lady with much that you are trying to understand about your life."

Payton looked at him as if to say, "What are you trying to say about me, especially since you don't know me?" *I'm getting a little tired of people trying to read me,* she thought.

"I know you are asking how I know when I do not even know anything about you."

Payton perked up and gave him a strange look, the same strange look she gave Lady Von Kisser when she tried to read her and did not even know her.

He smiled at her. "Every morning when I walk my grounds... First, Ms. Payton, what is your personal relationship with the Spirit?"

Uh, do you mean am I a Christian, Jew, etc.?"

"Yes, if you want to put it that way."

"I'm a Christian and have been since I was a little child."

"Humm," he said and nodded his head. "Again, every morning when I get up and walk my grounds, I am spending time with the Lord, connecting to Him so that I may be used as a vessel every day and to allow His will to be done within me. He has blessed me with so much in my life."

She interrupted and said, "Yeah, you think? Look around us."

He turned around to say, "Young lady, no, not the material things you see here. Please understand Satan can give you things, and his things come with much sorrow. He has given me peace that surpasses all understanding. I lived a life of substance. There was a time I lived a life of emptiness. My life changed with a spiritual divine intervention. I met someone who said 'no' to me. And that 'no' changed my life. I wanted something that this person was not willing to give. So, the challenge was on. I had never really experienced the word 'no' in my surroundings, but I wanted her."

"Her?" Payton asked.

He looked over to her with a little grin. "Yes, her." He gave her a look that said don't interrupt me anymore, so she didn't. "On my journey of trying to be with her, I met *them*: the Father, Son, Holy Spirit, and my destiny mate. She was the first woman who came into my life and re-introduced me to the Lord. I knew of Him. I just never believed who He really was until I started seeing him in her walk.

As she walked in his power and presence, it was something to see. Her confidence, peace, and desire to be so like him. Meeting her made me realize I did not have a relationship with the Lord. I was a walking carnal of flesh. You see, we associate spiritually with flesh. You think you are spiritual when you are just flesh in spiritual clothing. That's why so many just walk in works, and you don't see the fruits of the spirit. Because of her, I accepted the Lord as my personal savior again."

"So, you asked him back into your life again?" asked Payton.

"Yes, I rededicated myself to do what He predestined me to be. When the spirit came upon me again, I received the gift of the Holy Spirit. So, Payton, yes, the Holy Spirit has told me much about you. While you were sitting on the front stoop of my grounds, I asked the Lord why you were here. I also asked Him to allow me to be a vessel used by Him today. I do not believe in coincidence. I believe in divine connections. Ms. Payton, I could spend a lot of time talking to you about what the Lord has shown me. I would like us both to be on one accord. You have told me you were a Christian as a child, yes. But I need to know, have you ever verbally accepted the Lord as your personal savior, asking him to come into your life to be saved?"

Payton looked at him with a puzzled look on her face. She knew the answer was no because her holier-than-thou friend often spoke to her about her life and about accepting the Lord as her savior, but she would not because she didn't want anyone judging her when she did not live up to the standards of that lifestyle.

"No, I have not," Payton said to the Duke.

"Well, how has life been, trying to live on your own terms?"

Payton thought about it, and she knew she couldn't lie to him because he was a prophet, at least she thought he was by the way he brought up things about her that he could not have possibly known. "Not very well, Duke, not very well."

He smiled at her, and they continued the conversation. Payton agreed to accept the Lord as her personal savior right there at that moment. She could not believe she did it without much push. There was something about this moment, and she felt in her spirit this was the time to do this. Afterward, Payton stood there waiting for something to happen. Still standing, she opened her eyes, but there were no feelings, no stars, absolutely nothing.

The Duke could see the disappointment in her face, and he chuckled. "It was not what you thought it was going to be." He explained he wasn't laughing at her but for her. "I had the same experience. I thought it was going to be this major explosion. Let me assure you, Jesus is not a hoax encounter. People have different experiences—some feel things and some do not. Faith is not based on feelings, and the minute you start walking your Christian life based on feelings and not being led by the spirit of the word of God, you will experience a lot of defeat. You must look at your feelings as a young undisciplined child, Joyce Meyer says. You cannot let them control you. You must control them."

After some additional small talk, the Duke started in on a love journey of discovering himself that made him a better man for others. But he started imparting much knowledge to her about men and women relationships.

"What you are putting into your relationships has much to do with what you will get out of them. You do not just drift into a good relationship. Allowing a man to feel like a man means allowing him to walk and work in his God-given position. The head of the household if he is your husband is a good foundation to start on Ms. Payton. When this happens, there is nothing one will not do for his partner. You see young lady, people are with people because of the way they make them feel. That is why people often look at people who do not look as if they belong to each other in strange ways. You say, 'how in the world did he get her' or 'why is she with him?' Again, it has everything to do with what they bring out in each other. Also, always know your holes."

"Holes," Payton said with a confused look on her face. The other day, Dr. Tira Collins talked about the position. *These people on this side of the world have some strange analogies.*

He chuckled at her confused expression. "Please come."

They continued to walk the grounds. There was a long pause and a sigh. "Let's sit here a minute if you don't mind," he said.

"Of course," she said. If the truth is told, she was getting a little tired and kind of hungry.

"You must understand the authenticity of the relationship. Understanding your weakness and strength and vice versa with your mate."

Author's Note

"I have and always will be a hopeless romantic. Yes, I am 'the happy ever after' girl. That's me, and what made it escalate was when I saw *Rocky*. There was a scene in the cold meat room when Rocky was working out with the meat in the meat locker. He was speaking with his girlfriend's brother Pauly. Out of curiosity, Pauly asked Rocky what he saw in Adrian. There was no secret that she was not very appealing to the eyes. Adrian was plain and wore large glasses that covered most of her face. Rocky said 'Gaps. I have gaps, and she has gaps, and together we fill each other's gaps.' I thought that statement was so profound and had so much wisdom. So instead of using the word gaps, I use the word holes. So many of us have holes, whether it is abandonment issues, abusive issues, low self-esteem, or emotional disconnection. We all have holes that need to be filled. The issue here is that so many are with individuals who do not fill their holes or lives with what they have missing." As I said earlier, stop expecting others to fill the needs or holes that only God can fill.

"The key is to invest in people who fill your holes. Again, you cannot give what you do not have, and there begins the frustration of toxic relationships. How often do we see many individuals in unfulfilled relationships? Cheating, emotional, and physical abuse. Please let me make this clear: there is only one person who can fill the holes completely in your life, and that's the Lord Jesus Christ. Marriage is ordained by Christ, and we are to become one. Therefore, when each other's holes intertwine, they become one in a relationship or marriage."

"The focus is to invest in people who fill your holes. Once again, you cannot give what you don't have and that's the poison that leads to the frustration and toxic relationships. But you and I are fully aware that many marriages and relationships weren't brought together by the Lord. Even ones brought together spiritually still deal with holes."

Payton

Duke spoke, and Payton's mind drifted. She was thinking about all of her holes in many relationships.

"Ms. Payton," she heard her voice being called.

"Yes," she said as she came back.

They continued walking again as he admired his grounds. "As a woman, you should make sure you know your needs so you can identify your holes."

"Sir Duke, these grounds are massive. Do they ever end?"

There she was again, another statute. He stopped and gave it that look again. Yes, it came back to her, the same look Lady Von Kisser had. She knew it because she had never seen it before.

"You see young lady, the reason you see such admiration on my face when I look at this beautiful piece of clay is that this is my angel. She is the beat of my heart. She made me feel as if there was nothing in the world that I could not do or obtain. When I met her, my life changed and was never the same."

He continued with a beautiful love story of the two. *Where have I heard this story before*, Payton thought.

Things connected and she realized that she had heard a similar love story. It was a similar love story to the one Lady Von Kisser told her. She did not interrupt; she just let him continue.

"Speak life into your relationships. I mean prophesy to the men in your life. Help them to dream again. The world gives them many struggles; therefore, let them know you are on their side. Men will know sooner than later if they want you in their lives permanently. If you are with someone for a long period and they have not made an exclusive commitment to you, start questioning the process. Allow me to share this last knowledge with you, Ms. Payton. Too many times we allow our past to dictate our future. People say my ex-spouse did this, my coach did not let me, my upbringing was this way. No one is saying that you do not have these emotions or have the right to identify with them. If someone comes by and knocks you down by mistake or intentionally, that is on them, not your fault. However, if they pass by you a year later and you are still on the ground complaining about someone knocking you down, that is on you. Life, relationships, divorce, loss of a job, stifling career can all leave you broken. The character-building process comes out of what you are going to do now with your life. Are you going to stop trusting everyone, stop working, and stop loving? If you go to a restaurant and the food and service are just awful, do you decide that you will never eat food again or visit another restaurant? Absolutely not. So, you see how foolish it is to stop moving forward because of your past? Well, that is just what you are doing when you live in the past and play the blame game. There is no room for the past in your future," said Duke.

Further Notes from the Author

I can recall my very first job. I was working in the mall as a salesperson. I was so excited until I got fired. This is my side of the story. I had a friend who was walking outside in the mall, so I decided to step out of the store and engage in some deep conversation. Yeah, talking about nothing. I saw my boss observing my actions, but because there was no one in the store, I did not think anything about it. I came in the next day, and she proceeded to tell me they did not need my services anymore. I was appalled. How could they let me go, the great salesperson that I was? Mind you, I had sold nothing. I told my friends how wrong they were, and that I was going to sue. I never stopped to see what part I played in me getting fired. You must work to keep a job. I laugh when I think about myself and my development in life. If we would often take a step back and evaluate our experience in life, we would make better decisions as we move forward.

Reflection: Identify your Holes: and find someone that can add to your life instead of subtracting. Allow your husband to be the head of the household by making room for him.

Foundation

Author's Note

I have been a blessed child. I was born in another country (Germany) raised in the Midwest (Indiana). I come from a strong family foundation. The definition of family has changed over the years by society, but for my purposes, my mother and father have been together since the age of thirteen; they have been in each other's life for sixty-four years.

My father still takes care of his girls. My childhood memories were my father getting up early to make sure things were ready for the day. Growing up, we did not get into a cold car, and the house was heated up and ready for us when we got up.

My parents made sure we had money in our pocket and when we were sick, he took care of us. When I dated, friends had to meet my father first and see if it was ok for them to date us. To this day, these same characteristics still exist in my family. I knew how it felt to be treated with respect and loved. Therefore, I knew what to expect out of relationships. I always valued and loved me, so walking away from relationships that were good to me and not good for me was not a difficult task. By no means was my early years perfect and without challenges but the foundation was definitely there. This is not the story of many individuals today.

Relationships are incredibly challenging, and many require a great deal of work and maintenance. Even though you may not have had a great foundation by not having had the desired role models in your life, you can start today, right now, and start building that foundation. If certain people are missing in your life, adopt them. Call them your heavenly angels.

Reflect: What would your heavenly family look like? Who would you ask to be a part of your family? We so easily ask people to be our mentors. Do this by developing the foundation of your new story.

Payton

The Duke went on to explain, "Men want to be valued as much as women. We show our interest differently. True, we like challenges and being in control, but what many don't realize is that we want to be with someone we can just be ourselves with—not having to be a great expectation of all your dreams—just wanting to be with us. Again, we are with women because of the way they make us feel. Never forget that, young lady." Another cardinal flew past Payton, and she quickly turned to view the bird, she tripped on a branch, it was gone.

Payton did not realize something was wrong until she could hear her name being called, but she could not respond.

"Ms. Payton," Sir Duke called her name sternly.

When she finally came to, he stood over her. "Are you ok?"

Payton was confused as she was pulled off the ground. "What happened?"

"I'm not sure. When I turned around; you had passed out on the ground." As things came into focus, suddenly it was not Sir Duke she was talking to anymore. The quiet man she saw when she first entered the grounds appeared before her from nowhere. He had that same strange look. He walked away and then turned to look at Payton as if to say follow me.

As she gained her composure, she followed him. "Sir, where is the Duke?"

The man gave her another strange look, turned around, and started walking again. They came to another part of the ground, and this time, there was no denying something strange was occurring. They came to a bigger than life statue, and this time there stood two people holding hands looking from over a rail as if they were standing on top of the water; it was a beautiful sight. As she looked closer, it was Sir Duke and that same statue she saw all over the grounds. The man looked at her again as if he wanted her to come closer and read the plate on the statue. The plate read Sir Duke Lennard 1854 and Lady Von Kisser—. You could tell there was an ending date, but it was worn off. *This must be a family member*, Payton thought. His mother and father were the only things that could make any sense from this. Lady Von Kisser was from here or was it her family? Where in the world did the Duke disappear to? It was getting late and Payton needed to get back to the boat, especially to find Von Kisser and tell her that she had met some of her family.

Payton stood there thinking about what unfolded on the grounds today with Duke as she walked back towards the entrance. The groundskeeper walked far ahead of her as if to say keep following me, so she did just that. She was happy, sad, and simply confused as she left the grounds. Sir

Duke and Lady Von Kisser were the names on the face-less statues and that date was centuries ago. Besides that, she realized what a wealth of information and interesting people she had met on this trip. Much of it had been about relationships. Her relationships had all been so toxic in her life, and she started to feel like she was understanding why. It had to do with three people. *Me, myself, and I*, she thought as she headed back to the boat. *I hate I didn't get to say goodbye to Duke, but he just disappeared when she woke up, he was there and then nowhere to be found.*

I GET IT

After all that Payton had experienced going through all her encounters, she was ready, ready for implementing all that she had learned from the first time she had met Lady Von Kisser to now Sir Duke. She got it; she finally got it. Her journey was never about other people she worked with, the organization she no longer felt part of, the friends she disconnected with, or the ones who disconnected with her. The lovers that she gave all of herself, willingly and unwillingly left her empty inside. It was all about her and how she had developed herself on this journey of life. It was not about the love affairs she had with others but about the love affair she had never had with herself first. You see the first love affair we must have is the love affair with ourselves. She knew it was the final answer to all her situations. She couldn't wait to get back to Lady Von Kisser to share.

When Payton finally got back to the bus stop to get back to the ship, the last bus had left. The saving grace was that this was the final stop on the cruise until they left in the next two days headed back home. Payton was able to get a taxi. As the car headed back over the mountains to get back to the ship, she noticed the sun was setting. At this time of the day, there was something different there. A glow. Payton realized this was something she could not pass up, so she tapped the driver and asked if he would pull over to allow her to embrace the view, and he did so at her request. She sat there for a moment before she even took a breath. Her body would not move; it was if she were paralyzed. And then it happened—there it was. The sun stood still. It was so different. All of a sudden, a small tear fell from the corner of her eye. It was a warm tear, a tear of no remorse but a tear of calmness. A tear of cleanliness. It did not come from her emotions, but it came from her soul. She felt so pure. It was as if she was communicating with the sun that just stood still. "Lord what are you trying to tell or show me," she said.

Author's Notes

In my life, many situations have occurred that I know the Lord was talking to me and challenging me in my walk with him. One day, my life stood still. In 2010, I had started a business, an Emergency Management Company. My partners and I were pulling things together. It was growing, and we had procured close to 2.8 billion in MOU's. Scripture was given to me by my best friend Sandy. In the book of James, it's summarized that a faith that has not been tested cannot be trusted. It's during the trying times in life that our faith seems weak and sometimes absent; however, the Bible teaches that it is in God's design to refine His people like gold that is refined in the fire. John Maxwell understands and teaches this concept in his writings, knowing that our faith is strengthened and deepened by the tests and trials of life. However painful and contrary to our natural thinking, trials are good for us, at least from God's perspective.

Well, greed and ego came on the scene which led to a lack of trust. Needless to say, the company fell apart, and I was so disappointed. Let me say this footnote. The biggest disappointment was that I lost one of my dear friends because she got caught up in the madness more so than the business. For what does it profit a man if he gains the world and loses his soul? Nothing but emptiness. The company was there one day and gone the next. My heart stood still, my body stood still, and my emotions stood still. This was when the Lord took me through my transformation journey, but I like to pin it my tear-formation journey. Separation, Relocation, Isolation, Revelation, Evaluation, Elevation, Manifestation, and then there was the Celebration. The Lord had to start showing me my true self during these transformation periods and seasons in my life. Galatian 9:6 says, "Let us not become weary in well-doing; for in due season we will reap, if we faint not, and in Ecclesiastes 3, "For everything, there is a season, a time for every activity under heaven."

RELATIVES

Payton

While Payton stood there, she knew what her next step would be. She no longer would standstill in her life and instead, move forward spiritually and powerfully. No more drifting into who she wants to become; she would rewrite her love story, and it would start with loving herself.

When she returned to the boat, she couldn't wait to tell Lady Von Kisser all that she had learned about herself and life. As she walked up the plank to enter the ship, there was something different about the entry. It was as if she was falling again, this time not physically but falling in love again with self. She recalled how she felt when she started falling in love with her first boyfriend—the newness of it all and the excitement that it brought.

As she approached the front desk, she asked the concierge for Lady Von Kisser. The clerk looked at her in a very strange way, almost as if she were crazy. Payton felt it was just her imagination doing its own thing. It was at this moment all things changed and the real story unfolded. The young lady left the front desk and went to the back. Payton got a little irritated because the girl at the counter took an exceptionally long time. While standing there, Payton turned her back to the counter and rested upon it. It was at the moment her focus was centered in the area that she first met Lady Von Kisser, and that warm feeling brought a smile on her face. She could not wait to see her again and tell her all about her journey and what she had learned, most importantly about Sir Duke Lennard.

"Excuse me, excuse me." Payton jumped because she was engulfed in her great memories with Lady Von Kisser. It was the young lady back at the desk, but she was not alone. This old couple came from the back out of an office. They looked like they were a hundred years old, very fragile, and very petite. She thought it was rather strange, but the next couple of minutes and phrases would change her life.

"Ms. Payton, I would like you to meet Dink Henburg."

Payton said, "I don't understand. I asked for Lady Von Kisser's room number."

The couple gave Payton a very kind smile. "Young lady, we would like to assume that you have met her? Would you join us over here?" They pointed in the direction of where she and Lady Von Kisser met for the first time. Payton still thought it strange that she asked for Lady Von Kisser, and now she was in the presence of this couple who looked like they were still living in the 18th century. The woman wore gaudy jewelry and an outdated hairstyle, and he was a slow walking man who looked like he just walked out of a novel. Payton turned back and looked at the young lady like, 'This is not who I asked for.' She gave her a little smirk like, 'You will see.' So Payton walked behind the very slow couple until they reached their destination, which took them about twenty minutes.

"Would you please have a seat young lady? There is something we would like to share with you."

In Payton fashion, she felt like she was getting ready to take another journey, one that she was not sure she was interested in. Payton shared her encounter with Lady Von Kisser with the couple.

The couple shared their story. "My child, the Lord has given you a vision. Lady Von Kisser shared a great deal with you about her life and her relationships. Allow me to share a story that holds dear to my heart. While in her middle year of age, she met a man who would change the trajectory of her life. He traveled the seas, and his traveling was done on this ship. He was a kind and gentle man who had so much to give. He had many failed relationships because his definition of love was of provision; as long as he was providing the luxuries of life, he felt all women should be happy." This man starts sharing some things Sir Duke talked about.

As Dink spoke, his words seeped into her spirit. This was similar to a story that she had heard before. This was the story Sir Duke shared with her just a few hours ago, the man that she met on one of her stops. "Excuse me, sir."

"Yes, dear," Dink said, with a smirk on his face.

Payton told him about Sir Duke Lennard with the same story.

The elderly gentleman had a gleam in his eyes. "Yes, my dear, I know."

Payton gave him a strange look. "What do you mean you know?"

"If you would allow me to finish, it will all become clear to you."

You could imagine that Payton was fit to be tied and starting to feel a little disrespected that this couple acted as if they knew her. *Every time I meet someone on this trip, they act as if they already know who I am and what I have been through,* she thought. Although she wanted to share these thoughts, she didn't.

"The gentlemen during his travel met this amazing lady who showed him, unconditional love. Because she had been through so much in her own life, she had learned so much about herself before she met this gentleman. This man became intrigued and fell hopelessly in love."

"Excuse me, this story is getting weird. I know this story."

Again, he gave that same smirk and a look that was starting to irritate her. "Yes, that is because the story is about Lady Von Kisser. You see, Lady Von Kisser was my dear friend and someone I grew to love and respect dearly. I met her through Duke Leon who was my brother. I met Von when I visited her on this ship under some very heart-breaking and unpleasant times regarding my brother, who had a very bad accident on this ship. Duke found his con-nection with the Lord through the water. He felt so much peace within himself when he was near water. He wrote to me and told me about how he and Von would take many walks around the ship deck. In fact, that is how their bond with each other, and God grew so strong. One evening after dinner, Duke and Von took one of their evening walks, and he proposed to her. During this time, he shared with her about his wealth. You see, we come from a long lineage of shipyards and ship manufactures. This ship we are on was incredibly special to my brother because our father helped build this ship, which was the last one in operation. The owner of the ship would never sell it back to our family, so my brother found comfort in being aboard this ship because he felt our father's spirit here. My brother would walk the decks of the ship because he felt close to him and the Lord at the same time. My brother called me and asked me to draw up some paper for his will. He wanted to leave all his inheritance to Lady Von Kisser because he was going to marry her. He told me how he would exchange vows upon the captain's private deck. And that is exactly what they did. The captain and my brother became great friends, so he allowed them to get married at the top."

As Dink continued to talk, Payton could sense a mood change.

"You see, when Lady Von Kisser went back to the honeymoon suite, my brother took a walk around the top of the boat to reflect on his new union. He always felt so connected to the universe on the very top of the ship. So on this amazing night, it was no different. My brother wanted to be alone with his thoughts, my father, and God. The captain told me my brother did just that, went to the top. Then something happened that the captain said his eyes could never explain. As he left the top deck after the ceremony, he looked around and saw my brother walking away toward the bow of the ship. There was something so angelic about him that my brother appeared to glow. The sun was setting, and the image of my brother's body was the most beautiful thing the captain had ever witnessed of his traveling the seas. It was like the sun stood still. My brother turned around to look at the captain. My brother said this was the most spiritual moment he experienced in his life. He felt like he was in the presence of God. As my brother shared his experience with the captain, the captain's tears came streaming down his face This took him to another place. He said he had not shed a tear since he was eight years old back at his parents' funeral service. They were killed in an accident while out at sea. Water had his heart because he felt close to his parents. Water was a two-edged sword for the captain. It caused great pain, but it also gave great comfort. Their loss of loved ones is what bonded the captain and my brother. What the Captain was seeing and feeling took another turn. As he watched Duke walk to the top of the ship, the Captain dropped his head and wiped tears from his face. When he looked back up, Duke was gone. The captain said he called his name thinking he had walked to the other side of the ship. He hurried to make sure he was ok, and there was nothing. He tried not to panic but did after fifteen minutes of looking. To make a long story short, my brother disappeared into thin air into the sea."

Payton's body went still. "What do you mean he disappeared?"

Dink did not sound disturbed, so she did not know how to take it.

"Yes, my dear, he was gone never to be seen again."

"There was no body, nothing?"

"There were people out that evening on all levels. No one saw anyone fall from the top, nothing. It was like he vanished into thin air. The news was heartbreaking for Von. She had just married the man of her dreams, and now he was gone. She was so devastated over her loss that she made this ship her home. She never wanted to leave because she felt his spirit on the ship. When she inherited his wealth, she later purchased this ship and named it after him."

Payton's eyes grew wide and sad all at the same time because she felt such sadness for her new friend.

Author's Notes

In life, there will be many situations that we will never understand. Job 13:15 says, "Though He slays me, yet I will trust in him." I lost my brother in 1985. His tire blew out while in the car with our cousin. I could not understand why the Lord allowed my only brother not to survive. In my life's journey, I do know that there are things I will never understand. Never will I be able to comprehend the "Whys of our Lord." I will never understand why children lose their parents or parents lose their children at an early age or any age, or why there is so much pain. But all I must do is read through the Old Testament and see all the sacrifices that followers of Christ made. John the Baptist was beheaded, Steven stoned to death, and most of all, Jesus went through the torture and sacrifices for our sins. He was a perfect sacrifice by a perfect person to perfect some very imperfect people.

Payton

Payton could not move after this information. She thought about the stories Lady Von Kisser had shared with her: all the ups and downs with relationships, how she became not just a strong woman but a woman of strength, and how she became an overcomer and a lover of self. Now this, to lose the man of her dreams in such a horrific way and leaving an open wound of loneliness—a wound of not knowing where he is. After hearing all this, Payton stood and went over to the beautiful royal purple chair and took a seat. It brought back so many wonderful memories of their talks that day. After she gained her composure, she looked up into the eyes of Duke's brother and his wife. It was apparent that they cared dearly about Duke and Von by the passion that ran so deep as they shared this information with Payton. There was something different about them as they stood over her. It was as if they knew what her next question would be. When she opened her mouth, a voice came over the intercom of the ship. They announced that the Honorary Ceremony for Lady Von Kisser would begin in thirty minutes. "What is that?" Payton asked.

The couple smiled. "This is an annual celebration for the legacy of Lady Von Kisser and my brother. This is why we are visiting the ship today. We come every year in remembrance of my family."

As Dink spoke, Payton watched his mouth moving, but she could no longer hear the words. All she heard was, "In remembrance" and then the voices came back into play. "What do you mean in remembrance?" She became lightheaded. It was the same feeling she felt that night in Chicago when her life changed for the worse.

He smiled. "Please follow us."

Payton did so without knowing what laid ahead of her. Sometimes in life, we are given a perspective of information not fully aware of the total picture or meaning. There is a story and a story behind the story. As Payton continued to follow the couple, her eyes widened when she saw an amazing portrait of Lady Von Kisser, and there he was, Duke Leon on full display. "Is that Duke?" Payton asked with a confused look on her face.

"Yes, my dear, that is the portrait of them both. They took it to be displayed at the ceremony on their wedding day."

Payton's hands shook as all these flashbacks ran through her mind. Duke Leon had such a resemblance to Duke Lenard, the Duke who gave her so much advice about male relationships and the beautiful women he met who taught him a great deal about love. A thought passed through her mind. Could this be Duke and could the woman he was talking about be Lady Von Kisser? It could not be because Duke Leon is not living. *Uhm, Duke Lenard, Duke,* Payton thought. Payton shook her head because it was confusing and ridiculous.

As she walked closer, things took on a different light. "Wait, wait a minute. Wait, wait, wait," Payton said to Dink.

"Ms. Payton, no. You must wait. Sit and listen, and it will become plain to you. Sometimes the Lord just wants us to sit with him and allow him to reveal himself to us."

Making It Clear

As Payton sat in that chair, a beautiful love story of two individuals continued to unfold before her that made her heart melt. It was a love story she prayed would be her destiny to experience in her lifetime. Every time she met someone new in her life, she would think this was the one— the one who would add so much happiness, so much joy to her life. Sometimes she was afraid to give herself totally because she did not want to jinx the relationship. Most of the time, deep down in her heart, she knew it would not last. But what is a girl to do but hope? Because Payton sat in the back of the audience, she could not see where Lady Von Kisser sat. She desperately wanted to talk to her because she had so much to share with her about her transformational journey and all the encounters that she experienced. But most of all, she wanted to tell her about the man that she met who looked so much like her husband. She wanted to tell her about his amazing love story that mirrored her relationship with Leon and the family estate she visited. As her thoughts raced, something within her spirit told her to get out of her seat. She got up and headed to the front to become more engaged in the ceremony as if she were having an out of body experience. She walked to the front of the room. She heard a voice telling her to stop. To her amazement, her eyes landed on two empty seats, not just any empty seats but two royal chairs, a replica of the purple seat in the front of the ship. The seats had two beautiful flowers on them, the same violet broach that Lady Von Kisser wore when she first met her that day on the ship. Payton looked up at the speaker's angelic face. He had such a presence as if he stood on clouds. He looked at her and began telling the love story of Lady Von Kisser and Duke Leon. It felt as if he spoke only to her. As she looked around the room, she did not see anyone else at first, only she was present. That soon went away and suddenly she could hear and see who all were in attendance. "I need to see what I have been drinking back at my table when I get back because this is feeling strange," said Payton.

The speaker went on to say how Duke Leon was the joy of Lady Von Kisser's life. He completed her, showed her how to love herself first, and how she learned to have a love affair with herself for the very first time.

Most importantly, he spoke about <u>how she knew how to allow a man to be the man in a relationship without sacrificing her strength and contribution to the relationship.</u> Payton's heart was breaking and full of love and joy all at the same time. She felt so heavy and had no idea why. As she stood there trying to understand the heaviness she felt, she assumed Lady Von Kisser would make a grand entrance. Payton continued to stand in the aisle, wondering when they would bring out the guest of honor.

The next words that she heard coming from the podium were words that changed the trajectory of her life AGAIN.

"In the 18th century, Lady Von Kisser changed so many lives. The death of her husband on this day over 200 years ago left her with a broken heart but left us with a legacy of her spirit that continues to minister to the lost and broken hearts and souls of women across the world. Her spirit continues to linger in the decks of this vessel and continues to write love stories for countless women, many of whom are represented here tonight. Many have come back on this day to celebrate a woman, a queen who taught each one of them to love, but most importantly, how to have a love affair with themselves first."

Payton felt as if a foreign object pierced her lung and she gasped for air. "What in the world is going on?" Payton asked in disbelief. Women from everywhere stood and applauded. It looked like the United Nations in that room. Every ethnicity seemed to be represented. Some had men with them some had none. Another feeling rushed over her. *Who is playing with me?* she thought. She looked for Duke's brother and his wife, but they were nowhere in sight. Nothing made sense to her.

Suddenly, a warm wind blew over her face. A presence and a familiar smell settled over her. "Oh, there it is. I know that scent. It's hers." When she met Lady Von Kisser, she had an amazing scent, a biblical scent like myrrh and frankincense. It was as if she were still there hovering over. Payton turned toward the ocean to follow the scent.

Where is Dink? she asked herself, turning in circles to find anyone that she recognized. As she moved out onto the deck at a distance, her eyes fell upon a vision she knew well, a vision of her new friend Lady Von Kisser. She looked as if she were walking on water.

"Where am I, and what is going on? 18th century, am I in the 18th century? They said you are a spirit that travels the hall of this ship. What is going on? Oh my God. Ok, I'm dreaming. Lord, please wake me up. I'm ready to get up. This can't be happening to me." Payton realized she was beginning to have shortness of breath.

"Payton, Ms. Payton please wake up." As Payton was coming back in a conscious state, she could hear someone calling her. She opened her eyes. Dink stood there.

"Thank God, you are all right."

They stood her up and took her back inside to sit down to talk. "Young lady, you were a chosen one. Lady Von Kisser's spirit still lives on the ship, and it's evident again with you. That is why when you came to the front desk and asked for her, they came and got me. They knew her spirit and presence were here again. As Payton looked at him, he said, "I know my child, no you are not going crazy. Did you see all the other crazy women in the room?" He laughed. "The Lord works through his angels every day."

Payton had a question on the tip of her tongue, and he could sense it. "We don't know how she left this earth. On the first anniversary of Duke's death, she gave a ceremony just like what you witnessed. The many hearts they touched were present just like today. While the program was going on, we saw her get up and walk to the deck. The waiters went to see if she needed anything, and she told them no, she just needed to get some fresh air. She turned to me and nodded her head and gestured that she was ok. I responded with a nod, knowing she just wanted to be alone to reflect on memories of Duke. She stood there at the rail. I turned my head to look back at the program, and when I turned back around, she was gone. I thought maybe she walked down the deck. I did not think anything about it anymore. That was the last time I laid eyes on her."

Payton recalled that her scent came from the deck. A smile came over her face when she thought of her spirit out on the deck and hovering over the water. "I met Duke Lennard today and he looks just like Duke Leon."

"That is because Duke Leon's name is Lennard."

"Spirits. All of them have been nothing but spirits," is all Payton could manage to say.

The waiters saw her from the inside and rushed out to assist her. "Miss are you ok?"

"Yes, I think I am."

"We observed you talking to yourself and was wondering if everything was ok."

"Yes." She looked around and no one was there. *No Mr. Dink, no wife. No one. Again, as I said, spirits. All of them have been nothing but spirits.*" Payton said to herself.

REFLECTIONS OF THE DAY

As Payton laid in her quarters after everyone left or disappeared, she felt such peace in her spirit. But there was also loneliness because she wanted to talk to Lady Von Kisser; she wanted to share so much with her about her self-discovery to finding and understanding love, relationships, and most of all herself. Now it was all bottled up inside of her. A tear ran down her face. She wiped the tear away and the scent came over her again. It was Lady Von Kisser. This made her jump out of bed. "Lady Von Kisser is that you. I know now that it is you. Please, please let me see you. Please I need to feel you and talk to you."

Nothing happened for a while. Then she did something that she had not done in years. She started praying. She did not think she would remember how to pray because she had not done it in such a long time. But as a little girl, there was always something there an unexplained connection with her and the Lord. Payton could not recall when she stopped her fellowship with the Lord. But tonight, it came back to her. This time as she prayed, something amazing happened. She started praying in other tongues. She knew what this was because one of her dear friends told her about her experience of receiving the gift of the Holy Spirit. She could not stop. It was as if something took over her tongue. It was an amazing thing to experience. She felt as if the Lord had taken her by the hand and said, "Come up here with me and experience my presence in a way that you have never before," and that was what happened. Something pulled her strings. She got up, put something on, and headed to the bow of the ship. All of this became so clear as she ran as fast as she could. As soon as her tongues ceased, she knew exactly what to do.

"Ok, Lord I don't know why I'm going up here, but I do know you do." She had such peace in her spirit as she approached the top deck of the ship. "Yes, the area where the disappearance happened. Ok, Lord, you have me here. Now what?" Soon as those words came out of her mouth, it appeared as if an angel had touched her. Looking away from the ship, Lady Von Kisser was in all her glory. Payton did not move. It was as if the Lord himself had stepped down from heaven and presented himself before her. All she could do was take her hands and put them over her mouth so she would not scream.

"My child yes, it is I. It is I who came to see you, not the other way around. I know that you think you have been ordering your steps, but it is only of the Lord who gives us directions. You came to this place trying to find peace not knowing all along peace was within you. As you traveled the earth meeting different people who gave you insight, it was always the Lord working through them. I know you desire to tell me all, but I know all. I was always there. The small dog barking at the red cardinal. I was there. The women at your old corporate office, the red cardinal by the waterfall, and the red cardinal on the shoulder of my statue in the garden, that was me there with you the whole time."

"And Duke?"

He stepped from behind her and said, "That was me."

Payton jumped, screamed, and said, "Oh my God!" She wanted to turn around and run. "But how, but, but, how did you know about me?"

"God is omnipresent, and omniscient, omnipotent. He knows all, sees all, and is all-powerful. My child, He has had His hand on you all your life. When you were young, you asked Him to come into your life. He said He will never leave you nor forsake you. We move, He doesn't move, my child. Your life is predestined, and whatever He starts, He finishes. He does not make robots. You made choices and you made decisions to lean into your own understanding about your life. In Ecclesiastes, it summarizes that nothing physically touched the soul for the soul alone belongs to God. So, nothing you could have done in your life would have satisfied you because you were living a horizontal life and not a vertical life, focusing on what is under the sun rather than what is above the sun. You were leaving the Lord out of everything, and you see where that got you."

Lady Von Kisser stepped in and said, "As women, we must learn to value what the Lord has given us. He has given us guidelines to live by and an instruction manual for relationships, but we keep taking the pen out of his hand and writing our own narrative when things don't work out the way we desire them to. We want to jump ship and blame it all on the Lord. We wind up in empty relationships because we don't seek God first, allowing him to fill the right holes with the right mate. Without the direction of the Lord, we allow others to test drive us physically and emotionally and wonder why we don't have anything to fill within ourselves. My child, you were equipped with everything you needed because it was birthed when you were born. All the seasons of your life you went through was because God was developing you into the vessel he needed to complete what he predestined you to be. There is the call and the preparation for the call. No one is developed in the same manner. Your seasons are different from everyone else's; that is why some people bloom in careers and relationships at different stages in their lives."

Payton stood there in awe because this woman who entered her life was ordained by God.

"When you understand pain is a process of development, you will no longer see pain as bad. It becomes powerful to you. Look at the pain like a sore, scab, and then a scar. Many of the issues you have gone through in relationship have left scabs. They look like they have healed on the outside, but they have not healed on the inside. The sores are easy to see because they are still wounds; they are red, and you can still see them with the naked eye. The scars are healed. They may still hurt emotionally but not physically; they are evidence of what you have overcome. While you are learning how to love yourself again, stop validating who you use to be and focus on who you are now in relationships. Now go and rewrite your love story the way it appears to your knowledge. Write it in your love journal the way you want it to end. We have not because we ask not. Your journey on this trip was finding you, your love for yourself, and not receiving it from anyone but you and the Lord. Now you will never allow someone to treat you any kind of way other than through LOVE. Welcome to your first love affair with yourself, my Payton."

"We are proud of you, my child. You are now equipped to go out and teach the kingdom on what you have experienced. We will no longer be here, but you have the most precious one of all and that is the Holy Spirit. My work is done here; my journey is on to others who lack understanding in finding their value. I am a vessel that is being used by God, and now you will do the same. We wish you well my child." Lady Von Kisser and Duke held hands, kissed each other, and disappeared looking just like the last statue she viewed at the estate. So did Payton. She collapsed as Von Kisser and Duke Leon's spirit evaporated into the sea.

Here Again

When Payton came to, she heard voices around her and she felt heavy hands on her face. "Miss, Miss, are you alright?"

The voices were far away. When her eyes started refocusing, all she could see was the sky. Once her vision came back into focus, she finally became conscious. There were a lot of people standing around her. Coming out of her grogginess, she felt herself being pulled up off the ground and being placed on top of something.

She heard a familiar voice. "Payton, Payton."

When her eyes caught up with her vision and the sound of the voice, she saw it was River. "Baby, baby, are you ok?" he said in a panic.

"What happened?" Payton said.

"You fell and hit your head by this wall."

"Hit my head?"

"Yes. I just happen to be out—" He looked away in mid-sentence. "It does not matter. Are you ok? How do you feel?"

"I'm fine, I guess," Payton said. As Payton gained her composure, she tried to grasp all that was happening. She looked around and realized she was no longer on the cruise but back in Chicago. She was so confused and then it all started coming back to her. The last thing she recalled was when she was falling and hearing her man talking to another woman on the pier when he was supposed to be out of town.

"I guess you hit your head because you were out for a while. We called the ambulance, but you came out of it before they arrived."

"You mean it was all a dream?" she said under her breath.

People were looking at her, unaware of what she was saying.

"We're glad that you are ok," said all the people standing over her. The crowd started disseminating leaving only the two of them standing there. She could see his lips moving, but she was not hearing anything he was saying. He embraced her so hard that her mind and body started to go back to a place of falling in love with him. The good memories.

> *The thing that hurts us most is that when someone has hurt us, we tend to recall only the great things about the relationships.*

> *The key to a breakup is to remember why you broke up in the first place. People continue to go back into toxic relationships for many reasons, but one of the main ones is because of how people made them feel in the good times. Try recalling how they made you feel in the bad times. This will keep you true to valuing yourself.*
> - Patricia Y. McCullough-Oliver

So True!

Payton shook her head and said, "How did I get here again?" She closed her eyes and said, "Satan, get ye behind me."

Payton once again felt as if she was in a dream, but this time she was fully aware of what was going on and has been going on.

"Baby, I'm so glad that you are ok."

As he moved his lips, Payton's mind went back to her travels in her dream recalling all that she had become aware of, and all the words of wisdom she received along the way. At that very moment, that familiar scent flowed through the air. To her left sitting on the wall that bordered Lake Shore Drive was a red cardinal. This time she knew exactly who it was. It was her "angel" Lady Von Kisser. As she stood there, the Holy Spirit gave her some wisdom that came out of her mouth. Payton knew only the Lord Jesus Christ could have put this dialogue together. The words started flowing. The peace and calmness that came over her was proof for the first time that Jesus was living within her. The old Payton the FLESH that lived in her would have walked him over to the lake, pushed him in, walked away, and told no one where he was. Oh yea, she also would have stood there and watched him drown in the process.

Payton extended her hands, palm up in hopes he would take them into his. He did just that. Holding them for a while she gazed down at their connection and then moved her eyes up towards his. It felt as if it took forever for them to meet. This visual reminded her of the many things she fell in love with him. His strong, long physique, his beautiful green eyes. There was something different about them this time. They were not as beautiful as she recalled. What happens in life is when we discover how beautiful we are on the inside, all that we thought was beautiful in others on the outside no longer appears the way we once imagined.

"River, I want to bless you with a couple of things, but there is something that I want in return," she said. "Know before you give me your answer, these gifts that I will give you are priceless. No questions, just a yes or no."

He glared at her and noticed that there was something so different about her that he couldn't put his finger on, but he could not recall this beauty that he was seeing or this feeling that exuded from her. "Yes," he said hesitantly. "I will accept the gift." The words that came next out of his mouth were words deep down inside she wishes he had expressed to her so many times when her heart was with him. "I'm yours, baby. What is it that I can do for you?"

"There is nothing I would not do for you after watching you laying there on that pavement. The thoughts that I may have lost you gave me such a new perspective on us. I'll do it. I'll do it," he said fervently.

Again, hearing those words moved her spirit nowhere, but she was still rebuking the flesh silently. "There will come a time in your life where the spirit becomes so strong within you and set you free from so much bondage that you may not become aware of it until later. Then there will be a time when you will be living in the present when it occurs. I want you to open your mind and your heart to receive what I must share."

His eyes grew large.

"I want you to learn to live in your truth."

"My truth," he said.

"Yes, your truth. Your truth of untruth. Your truth of emptiness, loneliness, selfishness. You live in this life by disrupting and destroying others' lives without their permission. Your emotional disconnect in a relationship, personal and professional has caused many so much pain. You live a life of deception. You are not who you appear to be. You are a very handsome and alluring man until you open your MOUTH."

His eyes became so wide, and he wanted to be offended by her words, but something would not allow it.

Author's Notes

When the Holy Spirit is involved in any divine connection, he will put you in the right setting for individuals to receive what you are saying. That is why when I get up in the morning in my quiet time, I read the word of God and then I pray in my prayer language. The Holy Spirit will put individuals in my spirit and will give me a word and pictures for them. With the pictures, I can read the interpretations right away, and sometimes I must study the picture. The majority of the time, I will tell the individuals I do not understand, and they will say, I do. This gift of prophecy I have had for some time but never really walked fully in the gift. The Lord has talked to my spirit in my early years I just wasn't familiar with his voice. When I call and say you were in my spirit then continue to talk on the phone, people get quiet and often say, "Patty, that is a right now word. How did you know? I tell them I did not, but God knew. One of the phrases that I have adopted in my life is "Keep your spirit sensitized so that when the Lord is talking to you, you will hear his voice." The word says you draw nigh to him he will draw nigh to you. We should desire to have not just behavior modification but a heart transformation in our lives.

Payton

As she took his hand she said, "Today, I want to give you two gifts." As she spoke, she gave him a firmer handhold. By the look on his face, he felt it. "I want to introduce you to my new best friend, the Lord Jesus Christ.

The expression on his face changed into a smirk. "Oh yeah, I know him. I'm a Christian."

"So, you have accepted him as your savior?" Payton said.

"Yes, I was baptized when I was a little boy at my family church. I am a Christian and have been most of my life."

"Ok," she said, "that it is good to know. So, you have been living 2 Timothy 3:5 having the form of godliness but denying its power. So, you are like most, playing the Christian card. The word says you will know my people by the fruit that they bear."

After much dialogue, he decided to rededicate his life to Christ to be a better person not for others, but himself. He understood that his parents would be very disappointed in him if they knew his truth of how he treated others in his personal and professional life.

Then Payton said, "The second gift I want you to have is my forgiveness. You and I are over, but I'm giving you a clean slate. I forgive you for your dishonesty with me. I have already forgiven myself for allowing myself to see relation- ships for what I wanted to see and what I wanted others to see. I did not see your truth because I wasn't living my truth. I forgive you. I wish you well as you allow the Lord to continue to develop you in a true Christian walk so that you can be a vessel that the Lord can use in his Kingdom. You have hurt some of God's vessels as well as many of your counterparts and cronies. But I give you a THIRD chance with me. A third chance for me to watch you grow and become a man with a right heart and not just a good heart."

Payton walked away from that night with the presence of the Lord all over her. She felt a freedom that she had not experienced in such a long time. Payton realized that she was always hearing about Christ and haveing a foarm of being a Christian, but she was a fraud. Knowing this truth was good for Payton on this night of discovery. It is not the truth that sets us free. It is the truth that you know, set us free and set Payton free on this night.

<u>Author's Final Words</u>

I love you, Payton, and I love all the women that this story has blessed by hopefully seeing yourselves in some of the scenarios. I ask that you take your journal, rewrite a beautiful love story, your new love story, and give others in your life a THIRD chance like Payton.

Authors Prayer

Lord, this story I dedicate to all the women in my life and those who are no longer a part of my journey in this new season, by my choosing or their choice. I ask that you bless them all. Lord, I ask that you touch their spirit and soul to make better decisions in their relationships, spiritually, personally and professionally. I declare and decree happiness through their relationships, first with you and then others. Patricia Y. McCullough-Oliver

Amen,

THE END

REFERENCES

Tavris, C., & Aronson, E. (2020). Mistakes were made (but not by me): Why we justify foolish beliefs, bad decisions, and hurtful acts. Boston: Houghton Mifflin Harcourt.

Ortberg, J. (2014). The me I want to be: Becoming God's best version of you. Grand Rapids, MI: Zondervan.

Meyer, J. (2011). Living beyond your feelings: Controlling emotions so they don't control you. New York: FaithWords.

Johnson. K. (2018) EMERGE! Rise Up, Be Fearless. Take Possession of Your Purpose. Sinclair Scott Media and Publishing.